7/13 TG
9/15 GV MC

GUARDIAN AT THE GATE

In 1776, Mr Henry Fortune shot himself, leaving his impoverished family under the guardianship of Marcus Grant, a complete stranger. Although the widow and her younger children accepted Marcus's presence at Fortune Hall, the two eldest Fortunes caused problems. Simon rebelled in a manner which brought him close to disaster. His sister, Caroline, found difficulty in defining her feelings for Marcus — especially when she learned of his close acquaintance with the beautiful heiress, Alicia Dawes.

Books by Kathleen A. Shoesmith in the Linford Romance Library:

AUTUMN ESCAPADE
BRACKENTHORPE
ELUSIVE LEGACY
BELLTOWER

KATHLEEN A. SHOESMITH

GUARDIAN AT THE GATE

Complete and Unabridged

LINFORD
Leicester

First published in Great Britain in 1979 by
Robert Hale Limited
London

First Linford Edition
published 1999
by arrangement with
Robert Hale Limited
London

British Library CIP Data

Shoesmith, Kathleen A. (Kathleen Anne), *1938* –
Guardian at the gate.—Large print ed.—
Linford romance library
1. Love stories
2. Large type books
I. Title
823.9′14 [F]

ISBN 0–7089–5524–X

Published by
F. A. Thorpe (Publishing) Ltd.
Anstey, Leicestershire

Set by Words & Graphics Ltd.
Anstey, Leicestershire
Printed and bound in Great Britain by
T. J. International Ltd., Padstow, Cornwall

This book is printed on acid-free paper

1

When Mr Henry Fortune shot himself in the summer of 1776, he left behind a widow and five children, the eldest aged just twenty years old. He also left behind numerous debts. The untimely end of the owner of Fortune Hall, in the county of Yorkshire, was totally unexpected, save by that gentleman himself. Seeing no way of extricating himself from debt, he set pen to paper, had the documents duly witnessed by unsuspecting servants, then fired the fateful shot. For Mr Fortune, that was the end of his troubles. For his widow, Sophia, and their two sons and three daughters, it was merely a beginning.

After the funeral Mrs Fortune, together with her elder son, Simon, and her eldest daughter, Caroline, seated herself in the library of the Hall to hear the reading of the will. The lawyer, Mr

Augustus Hilton, seemed reluctant to begin and stood in need of prompting by Caroline, eldest of the Fortune children.

'The conditions set down here,' warned Mr Hilton, tapping a nervous forefinger at the will, 'are somewhat unusual. My — ah — late client sought to make the best possible provision for his family — a worthy aim, beneath these unhappy circumstances.'

Caroline, her fair good looks enhanced by the black of her mourning-gown, said chidingly:

'Come, Mr Hilton! Let us know the worst! What is to become of us all? Our father would scarcely have made an end of himself had all been well. Well — what exactly is to be our degree of poverty? Must Mama take in washing? Am I to hire myself out as scrub-woman?'

Her mother gave a moan of protest and dabbled ineffectually at reddened eyes with a minute scrap of handkerchief.

'My love!' she pleaded. 'Remember we have just buried your poor, dear Papa. I — I am sure he did what he thought he must do. Papa always knew best!'

Simon, Caroline's junior by but a year, rose impatiently to his feet and faced the lawyer.

'Well, Mr Hilton?' he demanded. 'What is this 'provision' made by our ever-loving parent? *He* is well out of the business but *we* wish to know if we must pack our bags and head for the nearest poor-house!'

Sophia Fortune moaned anew and Mr Hilton, a small spare man with a bird-like manner, gave a nervous cough. The Fortunes struck him as a singularly heartless set of mourners, but it was scarcely his place to reprimand them.

'It was Mr Fortune's wish that the family should remain here at Fortune Hall,' he began with a rush as if anxious to relieve himself of the knowledge of the contents of the will. 'However — there will be very little actual *money* left when the debts have been met. I feel it will be necessary to practise the severest of economies.'

Simon Fortune gave a hollow laugh.

'Economy is something for which we have never had any use,' he retorted. 'Come, Mr Hilton — I can see you have not revealed all.'

The little lawyer shook his head and bit upon his lip.

'You will not like it, young sir,' he warned. 'You see — your father has left you all into the care of an old friend and distant relative. Mr Marcus Grant is named in the will as your — er — your guardian — if you will accept him as such.'

Having delivered his news, the lawyer hastily withdrew from the room, announcing that he would return when the family had had an opportunity to discuss their position.

Mrs Fortune, Caroline and Simon stared blankly at each other for several long minutes. The bright, fair curls and blue eyes of her children were slightly faded in the mother but, all in all, they made a handsome trio in their mourning black. Caroline was first to speak.

'Mama — can an old friend of Papa's become guardian to an entire family?' she asked with slow bewilderment. 'Is it possible?'

'If there is to be no money, then how will this Grant fellow contrive any better than we would do ourselves?' queried Simon truculently.

'I do not even recall having *heard* the name of Marcus Grant before today,' said the widow fretfully. 'And if he is a distant relative of your father's, then I am sure that I have never met him! Surely I would know his name, at least, if he is a connection of ours? Oh, my dears! This is impossible! My poor, dear Henry must have been *intoxicated* when he made his will!'

'Papa did not drink,' said Caroline flatly. 'He merely gambled away his family's substance. Yes — I know — ' she forestalled her mother, 'I am lacking in proper respect but, it seems to me that Papa has taken the easy way out and left all of us to bear the unpleasant consequences.'

'Caroline!' uttered Mrs Fortune faintly. 'I believe I am about to suffer a *spasm*!'

'Oh, no you are *not*, Mama!' ordered Simon firmly. 'Mr Hilton is waiting for our decision. Do we accept the guardianship of this Grant person — or do we seek out an alternative solution to our unenviable position?'

Caroline stared from her brother to her mother and shook her head slowly.

'Is there an alternative solution?' she asked quietly. 'If we bow to Papa's last wish, then we will at least remain together as a family — *and* beneath our own roof. The plan has much to commend it. I suggest that we let Mr Marcus Grant come! Let him manage our affairs, *but* we will not allow him to interfere with our lives. He may merely handle our accounts and our economy! Come, Simon, do you not see the sense of it?'

Sophia Fortune's brow cleared and

she waited hopefully for her son to reply.

'Caroline speaks good sense,' she said. 'What do you say, Simon, my love? I think your sister has put the matter into proper perspective.'

Simon frowned a moment longer, then he nodded.

'Let the fellow come,' he agreed. 'Doubtless he is middle-aged and set in his ways and will leave us to live as we please. As long as he can solve our financial problem then, I for one, will not grumble!'

The lawyer was duly invited to return and listened to the decision of the Fortune family without surprise. To his way of thinking, they were lucky that a saviour, in the person of the unknown Mr Grant, existed. Mrs Fortune was totally unsuited to coping with the burden of Fortune Hall — even had there been no financial worry. Under the existing circumstances, only a miracle, in Mr Hilton's opinion, could save the Fortunes from being parcelled off piecemeal to the unwelcoming hearths of less penurious relatives.

'I will set matters in hand,' said Augustus Hilton. 'First — Mr Grant must be apprised of the situation. There is, of course, a possibility that he may decline the — ah — honour.'

'*Decline*?' echoed Mrs Fortune. 'How can this Grant person dare to decline to carry out my poor, dear Henry's dying wish? Why, the fellow has no alternative but to come to our aid. It is his *duty*!'

'Ah — quite so, ma'am!' agreed the lawyer hastily. He could not bear 'scenes' and had had a full sufficiency of the Fortune family. 'I will contact Mr Grant and trust I shall bring you a favourable reply in the very near future.'

The door had scarcely closed behind Mr Hilton when Simon retorted forcefully:

'Pompous old windbag! Well — let us sit back and await Marcus Grant's pleasure!'

'There is little else we can do,' agreed

his sister wryly. 'I suppose we had best explain to the children about our peculiar situation. It scarcely matters what David and little Paula think, but Nico will not like it above half!'

* * *

The horseman reined in at the West Lodge gates and frowned disapprovingly at further evidence of disrepair. The lodge was evidently uninhabited, for its windows were cracked and curtainless and its roof lacked several slates. What should have been a tidy small garden to the rear of the lodge, was a miniature wilderness. The drive of unraked gravel was dotted at intervals by ragged tufts of grass. The gates were closed and tied together with frayed cord.

The rider's frown deepened. He turned his mount and urged it around the outer wall of the estate, coming to a halt when another entrance was reached. The South Lodge appeared to be in only a slightly better condition and a slatternly-looking woman could be seen through its open doorway, two young children hanging on to her skirts.

The gates were open and the drive was more or less free of weeds, but still the stranger frowned. He had spent the morning in visiting the estate's two farms, taken luncheon in a village-inn and was now nearing his final destination. He had seen nothing at all to please him that day and inclination urged that he should return home before he accepted involvement in the affair. It was not too late to bow out gracefully, he mused hopefully.

Suddenly a child ran out of the lodge and into the drive. At the same instant a black horse thundered into view, making for the gates. Powerless to avert catastrophe, the stranger saw the black horse rear sharply, its hooves only inches from the shrieking child. The rider was thrown into the bushes and the horse careered madly off through the gates and out of sight.

Dismounting, the stranger made haste towards the child who lay screaming and kicking upon the gravel. However, the woman from the lodge reached the boy first and snatched him up, shaking him as a terrier might shake a rat.

'Get back in t'house, you little varmint!' she yelled, releasing the child with a vicious slap. Turning to the stranger, she scowled and snapped: 'T'gates are open, sir. If you've business up at t'Hall, then ride straight in. I've enough on my hands wi'out acting as gatekeeper.'

The man gave her a look of extreme distaste then moved past her and went towards the bushes.

'Wait!' he rapped as the woman turned to go. 'I may need your assistance.'

Lying in a crumpled heap behind the bush was the ominously still figure of a youth clad in breeches and cap. As the stranger put a gentle hand on the unconscious brow, the cap rolled off and revealed untidy fair curls.

'Oh — 'tis Miss Nicola!' gasped the woman. 'What happened to her, then?'

'Her horse reared to avoid your child and she was thrown,' said the man shortly. 'Now — make haste up to the Hall and fetch help. The young lady is deeply unconscious.'

Moaning that it was not her fault that the accident had occurred, the woman obeyed and left him. He crouched beside the fallen girl, noting the way in which one arm was twisted beneath her body. So this was Nicola, third eldest of the Fortune family, he pondered. When the girl began to stir and groan with pain, he took her uninjured hand gently in his.

'Lie still, little one,' he advised softly. 'Help is on its way.'

Nicola Fortune's blue eyes filled with tears, blurring her vision of the tall, dark gentleman at her side.

'I — I fell!' she whispered disbelievingly. 'But — *why*? I ride as well as any boy.'

'Now, hush!' soothed the gentleman. 'It was not your fault. Ah — I hear someone coming.'

He rose to his feet at the return of the woman from the lodge.

'I've brought Miss Fortune and Mr Simon,' she muttered, then made good her escape.

Caroline fell upon her knees beside her sister while her brother stood there helplessly.

'What must we do, sir?' asked Simon shakily of the stranger. 'Is Nico going to — to die? Mama swooned when she heard the bad news.'

The dark gentleman's lips set in a thin line. With an impatient frown, he bade Simon mount his own horse and ride in search of the village doctor. Then he ordered the white-faced Caroline to return to the house and apprise everyone of what had occurred.

'We will need a hurdle on which to carry her,' he rapped. 'Come — pull yourself together, girl! Go quickly! Oh — send a servant in search of your sister's runaway horse. It will not aid her recovery to think her mount is missing. Go! I will stay with her for we must not move her until the doctor arrives.'

Alone once more with the moaning half-conscious Nicola, Marcus Grant acknowledged wryly that the die was cast. It was now too late for him to retire from this imposed guardianship. If ever any family needed guidance, it was this helpless, *hopeless* Fortune family! He had no alternative now but to accept the strange terms of Henry Fortune's will.

* * *

According to the village doctor — a brusque individual unused to being called upon to minister to the 'gentry' — Nicola had sprained her wrist and cracked her collar-bone. When everything possible had been done for the injured girl and she lay in a semi-drugged condition in her bed, Marcus Grant announced his identity and suggested that the other members of the family should assemble to discuss the situation.

When Mrs Fortune realised that *the* Mr Grant had arrived, she made a speedy recovery and came quickly to the library, untidily dressed in a loose wrapper, which caused the visitor to raise a frowning brow. Simon sat aloof from the others, flipping over the pages of a book in a petulant manner and Caroline's lips set in a mutinous line as Mr Grant began to outline his plans for them. Scarcely had he begun to speak, when the door opened and a shrieking little girl of tender years ran in, followed by a thin dark-haired boy with a pronounced limp. A red-faced nurse-maid hesitated in the doorway, twisting her white apron in nervous hands.

Marcus Grant's frown deepened as he waited for Sophia Fortune to restore order. However, she only flapped a helpless hand towards the youngest of her brood and it was Caroline who finally bade the children sit and be quiet. She then dismissed the nursemaid and closed the door firmly.

'Please continue, Mr Grant,' she said quietly. 'Now you have the whole family before you, so let us hear the worst.'

Marcus Grant waited until she had returned to her seat, then looked first at the solemn little boy, David, then at Paula, a chuckling, irrepressible five-year-old. He sighed heavily.

'First,' he began, 'I must make it clear to you that I am *not* the guardian Mr Fortune had in mind! That honour was intended to rest upon the shoulders of my father, who is also named Marcus. However, he is in indifferent health and sent me to decline the guardianship of his old friend's family. That was my original intention but I have changed my mind. I intend to take on the task in his stead. I must admit that the circumstances are unusual, but I will do my utmost to bring a little order to your lives.'

When he had left the room, the family sat in stunned silence, which was soon broken by a furious Simon.

'The pompous, mannerless boor!' he raged. 'Mama — do you agree to this — this disgraceful situation? Why did you not give the fellow his marching orders?'

Caroline drew in a deep, steadying breath.

'I had at least expected that Mr Grant would be an older man and someone we could respect,' she said, her blue eyes still wide with shock. 'But, Mama, this — this *person* is impossible! He will delight in making all of us jump to his command!'

Little Paula spoke next and they all glared at her.

'Will the nice man come back?' she asked innocently.

David was solemnly silent in his usual manner, his dark hair emphasising his total dissimilarity to the rest of his family. There was another brief pause before Sophia Fortune replied to her offspring.

'My dears,' she said, spreading her

hands helplessly, 'I fear we must bow to the inevitable. I admit that Mr Grant is rather young for the task, but he appears to be a very capable person and of forceful opinion. Do recollect that we are in a precarious financial state. What little money remains to us must be used with extreme care. Perhaps Mr Grant may prove to be our answer, after all! Unless we accept his terms, I am afraid that Great-Aunt Martha will be the only alternative and living under *her* roof would not do at all. Consider my *nerves*, my loves!'

Caroline eyed her parent with undisguised dismay.

'Do you mean to tell us that Great-Aunt Martha has offered to house us all?' she breathed incredulously. 'But — she likes no one but David, because he is so quiet. She positively *hates* Nico and puts up with the rest of us with a very ill grace. How odd that *she* should offer to take us in!'

'She considers it her Christian duty,' admitted Sophia Fortune unhappily, 'and will remind us hourly of the gratitude we owe to her.'

Simon pulled a long face.

'Very well,' he said at length. 'Does Mr Grant return next week? Ah — yes, I thought so. Well, let him come. Let him order our lives and keep the purse-strings, but if he tries to interfere in *my* comings and goings then we will really see who is in charge of this family. Remember — I am now head of the household!'

'Are you, dear?' asked his mother vaguely. 'Ah, well, Mr Grant does not seem a bad sort of person, after all. No doubt a heart of gold beats beneath that cool exterior!'

'I very much doubt,' said Caroline evenly, 'that he has a heart at all. I know that I have taken him in intense dislike.'

'Take him or leave him, my love,' said Sophia Fortune, 'but make no doubt about it — Marcus Grant will be here to stay!'

2

Within two weeks of Mr Grant's visit, workmen arrived to repair and renovate the West Lodge for his personal use. Too late, Simon made his protest at having the family 'guardian' living upon the very doorstep.

'But, my dear, it seems a very sensible idea,' defended Mrs Fortune. 'Naturally, Mr Grant did not wish to encroach upon our privacy by taking up residence in the Hall itself! I think he is showing a fine degree of sensibility by keeping himself at a distance. In any case, he will not be living *continually* at our gate. He will use it for his visits here. And, after all, Simon my love, this is all to our advantage! The cost of the repairs to the West Lodge are being met by Mr Grant himself. The benefit will be ours, when you are one and twenty and he is no longer with us!'

'The whole affair is none of his business,' seethed Simon. 'Mama — his *father* was Papa's friend. Papa would not have intended that *this* should happen! Grant is taking far too much upon himself already and I am sure he is exceeding what is absolutely necessary. I questioned the workmen and learned that they are to move their paint and plaster to the South Lodge, once they have finished at the West entrance. Bassett will not like having *his* home turned upside-down.'

Before very long, it became clear that Marcus Grant intended that the slovenly Bassetts must go. Simon's fury knew no bounds when his mother calmly agreed to having her lodge-keeper, his wife and children moved into a cottage in the village.

'It will scarcely add to our consequence to leave the gate unattended,' stormed her son.

'My dear — we cannot *afford* to regard our consequence!' pointed out Sophia Fortune comfortably. 'Mr Grant is redecorating the lodge and will then seek a suitable tenant.'

'A *tenant*?' echoed Caroline, her amusement at her brother's ireful expression fading. 'Oh, no! We cannot have strangers living at the gates, Mama! Surely you have not agreed to this — this infamous plan? You are letting Marcus Grant ride roughshod over us all. Indeed — you are *abetting* him!'

Her mother was silent for a long moment, then she sighed.

'Consider, my dears,' she asked pleadingly. 'A tenant at the lodge will mean a regular rent flowing into our coffers. Mr Grant's main aim is to make the estate earn enough to keep us all in modest comfort. I cannot see anything to quarrel with in *that*. If you do not like Mr Grant's methods, then hold your tongues and look to the future. His guardianship is to last but two years. In that time there is every chance that he will have made us self-supporting.'

Caroline wrinkled her nose derisively.

'You make it all sound like a commercial enterprise,' she said. 'I hope I will not be expected to cultivate vegetables and set up a stall at the gate to sell them. The village people would think it a great joke to see me humbled in that way.'

'Depend upon it,' said Simon darkly. 'Grant will want something out of this affair for himself. After all, why should he dip into his own pocket *and* give up so much of his time to a set of strangers? I do not like the smell of it!'

'Then pray hold your nose, love!' retorted his mother. 'I intend that we should give Mr Grant a chance to help us. As to his motives — why, not everyone is mercenary. He wants to help us simply because he knows it is in his power to do so.'

'Very noble of him, I am sure,' replied Caroline bitterly, then with a lift of her brow she added to her brother: 'Come, Simon, we must talk this out together.'

Sophia Fortune frowned unhappily after the retreating figures of the eldest of her offspring. Why must Caroline and Simon be so difficult, she wondered fretfully. They would achieve no good purpose by attempting to thwart Mr Grant. But, she thought, brightening a little, Grant was not a man to be set from his stride by mere children!

* * *

Marcus Grant took up residence in the West Lodge in the third week of July. By this time, Nicola was upon her feet again, her arm swathed in a linen sling to rest the injured collar-bone. When she announced her intention of calling upon the new arrival and wishing him welcome, she met with fierce opposition from her elder brother and sister.

'But, Caro — Simon,' protested the astonished Nicola. Her sojourn upon her sickbed had shielded her from her family's divided opinion upon the new guardian. 'Mr Grant cared for me when I was thrown. Mama said he took complete charge of the situation and even had my poor Hermes caught and brought back to his stable. Why — Mr Grant is a *hero*! I intend to go and thank him immediately. I *must*, must I not, Mama?' she appealed, turning to her mother.

Sophia Fortune frowned at her two elder children.

'Certainly it would be proper for you to thank Mr Grant for all he did for you, my love,' she agreed firmly. 'He is to deal closely with our affairs and it would be foolish indeed for us to remain bad friends with him. Take the children to the West Lodge with you, Nicola. Then Mr Grant will realise that the *majority* of this family approve of him. He knows already that *I* am prepared to welcome him,' she added with a quelling frown at Simon and Caroline.

An unexpectedly heavy shower of rain postponed Nicola's visit to the lodge but did not prevent Mr Grant from paying a call upon Mrs Fortune that same afternoon. His courtesy-call was made with a complete lack of ceremony and he had left the Hall before the younger Fortunes were even aware of his arrival.

Marcus Grant returned thoughtfully to the West Lodge and was received at the door by Quimby, his manservant.

'Well, Mr Mark, sir,' said the man, divesting his master of a wet top-coat, 'we shall have our work cut out in this new venture, or I am much mistaken. To my way of thinking, this place has been let go to rack and ruin and the family do not even seem disposed to pull in our direction. I hope it does not all prove too much for us.'

Marcus Grant quirked an amused eyebrow at his manservant's serious tone, then smiled.

'Perhaps we may even come to like these Fortunes, you and I, Quimby,' he said lightly. 'They are helpless and feckless to my way of thinking, but perhaps they only need guidance.'

The older man gave vent to a sound suspiciously like a snort.

'They'll resent you at every turn, Mr Mark,' he warned, with the freedom of long acquaintance. 'After all, you are not renowned for your tact, sir.'

'That all remains to be seen, Quimby,' said Marcus enigmatically.

When Nicola visited the lodge next morning with David and small Paula she was followed, to her surprise, by both Caroline and Simon. Scarcely had Mr Grant received the three younger Fortunes into his small square sitting-room, than Quimby, his expression betraying nothing of his thoughts, announced the arrival of the two elder members of the family.

'Ah — so here you all are,' Marcus Grant greeted them blandly. 'It is good of you to come to bid me welcome. I was not sure you would receive me so happily. I am pleased to realise my anxiety was rootless.'

Simon forgot himself so far as to scowl and Caroline dug a warning elbow into his side. They had not planned to be openly antagonistic. Without so much as the flicker of an eyelid, Marcus Grant observed the whole of it. He wondered why Caroline should be so determined to dislike him. Simon's resentment was only to be expected. The lad was nineteen and fancied himself to be head of his family. Small wonder that *he* was not prepared to accept the interference of an outsider.

Caroline and Nicola were very much alike in looks, thought Marcus Grant, taking advantage of Quimby's bringing in fruit drinks for the younger visitors, by scrutinising the Fortunes closely. Both young ladies had fair complexions, golden curls and bright blue eyes but, where Nicola's expression was one of friendly, lively interest, Caroline's eyes were veiled and guarded.

Small Paula, greatly similar in looks to her sisters, was chatting freely to Quimby as she sipped at her fruit-cup. David, his dark looks making him appear something of a changeling in this golden family, gripped his glass tightly in both hands, neither drinking nor speaking.

Marcus Grant, observing the scowling silence of Simon Fortune, went out of his way to be pleasant to the young man, asking him if he would take a glass of wine. Somewhat sullenly, Simon agreed. When Marcus asked the young ladies their choice of refreshment, he met with a stony refusal from Caroline and a merry laugh from her younger sister.

'I am not yet sixteen and Mama would suffer a spasm if I asked for wine,' chuckled Nicola. 'I will take fruit-cup, please, sir!'

When he had met the needs of all, Quimby surveyed them morosely before leaving the sitting-room. Why that Mr Simon and Miss Caroline had troubled to come at all was hard to see. If anyone ever intended upsetting his Mr Mark it was those two, decided the manservant grimly. Well, he thought, we are on our guard and we can deal with the likes of you with our hands tied behind our backs.

The visit to the West Lodge was

scarcely a success, but Nicola seemed ignorant of the fact and chattered gaily to Caroline as they made their way back up the drive to the Hall.

'He's *nice*, isn't he, Caro? I told you that you must like him better when you met him properly. He is quite handsome too — but in a strong way — not *pretty* like that odious Hubert Channing.'

Caroline's set expression froze even further. The 'odious' Hubert was the sole suitor to her hand who had not faded from view upon her father's scandalous end. The Channing family, however, were far from wealthy and it was unlikely that Sophia Fortune would favour a match between Hubert and her eldest daughter — even had Caroline liked her suitor rather more.

'You may call Hubert 'odious', Nico,' she said, her nose in the air, 'but it could never be said that he smelled of the shop like your precious Marcus Grant!'

Nicola's eyes opened wide with shock.

'Caro — how unlike you to be so

spiteful and what an unfounded remark to make! Mr Grant is a proper gentleman and his family name is old and well-respected. There is not the smallest suggestion that they have ever had any connection with *trade*. I have been asking Mama about him.'

It was Caroline's turn to stare. She stood still on the drive while Simon and the children went on ahead.

'Mama did not even know the name of Grant before Papa's will was read,' she said coldly. 'Nico — you are making things up to suit yourself.'

'No, I am *not*,' retorted Nicola. 'Mama *did* remember later that Papa once had a friend called Mark Grant. Well, he is old and ill now and his son has come to help us out of friendship to our father's memory. You are being *horrid*, Caroline Fortune, and I shall not listen to you!'

Thus speaking, Nicola marched on ahead, leaving her sister to her thoughts. Marcus Grant had *bewitched* the entire family, with the exception of herself and Simon, pondered the unhappy Caroline. Well — time would tell, she thought forebodingly. Marcus Grant had already disturbed the pattern of their lives and she doubted that his future plans would allow either peace or freedom of choice for any of them.

3

'Simon, my love,' said Sophia Fortune at the breakfast table one morning, 'I would like a word with you in the library later.'

'If it is about that Grant fellow, you may save your breath, Mama, for I am not prepared to listen!' retorted her elder son gracelessly.

Sophia pursed her lips and frowned at him.

'You are being both rude and childish,' she said severely. 'I will not have this incivility from you, Simon, either towards myself *or* Mr Grant. Pray finish your breakfast and then come immediately to the library!'

With that she left the dining-room, closing the door forcefully. Simon turned and stared open-mouthed at his sisters. Caroline merely returned his look then gave her attention to the food upon her plate. But Nicola set down her knife with a clatter.

'Simon — you are horrid!' she said fiercely. 'Why not think, instead, of all the good that Mr Grant has done for us already?'

Simon scowled and was silent but Caroline spoke at last.

'Very well, Nico!' she invited. 'Pray give us your list of Mr Grant's good works. Come — you have our undivided attention!'

Nicola gave her an uncertain look then tossed her fair curls.

'Well — he was the only one to show sense when I had my accident,' she began. '*You* would have let me lie there forever!' She thought for a moment then went on: 'He has got rid of those idle Bassetts and is to bring in money for us by letting the South Lodge. He has given poor Mama a — a sense of *purpose*. Why — before he came she did not rise early enough to take breakfast with us and she did not trouble to *dress*! He is living in the West Lodge so that he is near enough to help us.' Nicola paused for breath, then rushed on: 'He has done so much for us, in so short a time, yet you will not even show him common courtesy, Simon and Caroline! I am ashamed of the pair of you! Well — I like him and would be proud to call him my friend!'

She stormed from the room almost in tears. Simon's scowl deepened.

'She is besotted with the fellow!' he sneered. 'Well, I had best go to the library and listen to Mama's grumbles.'

Left alone, Caroline toyed with the remainder of her food. Unhappily, she wondered if Nicola were in the right. After all, Mr Grant had done nothing to merit dislike, except by showing a certain scorn for their way of life. This burden of guardianship had not been intended for his shoulders. He could have denied responsibility. *Then* what would have become of the family?

Suddenly Caroline was uncertain of herself. Was she being totally unfair in being antagonistic? Simon's complete, almost reasonless, prejudice against Marcus Grant had found a willing echo in herself. Yet, she could still recall the withering look bestowed upon her by the family guardian, when she stood so helplessly beside her fallen sister that day. Nico was right — she had done nothing to help! It was evident that Mr Grant held a very low opinion of her. It was also obvious that he would be at hand for two whole years, until Simon attained his majority. Did she wish to be his enemy, or at best, his bad friend for so lengthy a span of time? Yet — short of suddenly beginning to fawn for his approval — what was she to do? Showing the least shade of favour towards Grant would bring the full force of Simon's scorn upon her head, she thought unhappily. Must she make a choice between the guardian and her own brother?

Leaving her breakfast unfinished, Caroline wandered over to the window and stared despondently out at the overgrown shrubbery. Everything had deteriorated recently, she admitted. Doubtless, Mr Grant blames the condition of the garden upon *me*, she thought wryly.

From the window she had a view of the drive, partly obscured by bushes. Suddenly, Simon came into sight, striding away from the house, anger evident even from his backview. As Caroline watched, Marcus Grant appeared, following Simon but at his own pace. Lost in conjecture, Caroline turned with a start when the dining-room door opened.

'Ah, so you are still here, dear,' said her mother brightly, coming over to the window. 'Simon is to ride to inspect the farms with Mr Grant. Nicola is helping Whitton with the horses and the children are at their lessons with Bessie. It is a fine sunny morning! Perhaps you would help me to tidy the roses upon the terrace, my love? I am sure that *ours* should not be the only idle hands about the place.'

Utterly bemused by her mother's firmly

pleasant manner, Caroline meekly followed to don an old gown and a shady straw hat. As the roses were in a somewhat wild state, Sophia Fortune also decided that they must wear stout gloves.

'Mama,' said Caroline at length, as she paused to disentangle her skirt from a thorny tendril, 'you did say that Simon has gone to the farms with Mr Grant, did you not?'

Her mother sighed and set down the blooms she had cut for the drawing-room vases.

'According to Marcus, the farms are running at a loss,' she confided.

Caroline's blue eyes widened.

'*Marcus?*' she gasped. 'You use his first name, Mama?'

'Why, yes, dear,' agreed her mother comfortably. 'He decided it would be foolish for me to continue to 'Mr Grant' him and, after all, our families are distantly linked.'

'Oh,' said Caroline blankly, 'and what does *Mr Grant* feel should be done about the farms?'

'He has plans,' confessed Mrs Fortune, 'but feels Simon should have some say in the matter. Whatever you may think, love, Marcus has no intention of being high-handed!'

They worked upon the terrace until well after noon, for the most part in silence. Caroline marvelled anew at her mother's energy and interest in the task and was at a loss how to treat this new, uncharacteristic decisiveness. They were still alone when they partook of a light luncheon of fruit and coffee in the dining-room — a meal her mother normally ignored.

'It is amazing how a little exercise sharpens one's hunger, is it not, dear?' observed Sophia cheerfully.

Caroline nodded abstractedly as she peeled an apple.

'Mama,' she said at length in a quiet voice, 'you like Marcus Grant very much, do you not? Are you angry with me? Do you judge me for not making him welcome? Nico is strong in his praise and rails on at me for my manner towards him. Yet how can I like him when he makes no secret of his disapproval of us all?'

Sophia Fortune turned and looked her daughter straight in the eyes.

'He is a fine, dependable young man, my dear,' she said softly. 'If I had my way, he is the kind of man I would choose for you! No — do not frown and look away, love! If he disapproves of you, it is because he does not know you properly. You could do far worse than Marcus Grant! If, eventually, he should approach me to ask for your hand, what would your feelings be then? After all, he is of an age when he should be thinking of marriage. You would make him a most suitable wife, my love, and you have the advantage of knowing he will remain in this vicinity for two years! Surely two years should be enough for — '

'Mama!' interrupted Caroline, her cheeks first white then red. 'Mr Grant does not like me. He makes it clear he has no opinion of me at all. Why should he take the drastic step of offering *marriage*? Oh dear — only *you* could have so foolish a notion!'

'Ah!' nodded Sophia. 'Foolish? Yes, I have been foolish in many ways, Caroline! I should not say it, love, but your father was a charming spendthrift and a gambler and I never attempted to change him. But now I am alone and I am determined to mend my ways! With the help of Marcus, it may be possible for us to *survive* with dignity. I wonder how he and Simon are faring together?' she added, every vestige of optimism fading from her tone.

* * *

It was a fine summer morning and, in the normal way, Marcus Grant would have enjoyed a leisurely ride about the Yorkshire countryside. The distant hills were now still green or brown but soon they would bear the purple glory of moorland heather. The sun was high in the cloudless sky and, somewhere overhead, a skylark was singing with its own inimitable pure sweetness. Looking up, Marcus caught sight of the small dot in the heavens which was the hovering lark. Then, turning to view his silent companion who was riding sullenly alongside, he suppressed a sigh.

Simon Fortune had agreed to come with him, but with a very ill grace and no small show of reluctance. Farms were not much in his line, he had protested.

'This estate is your heritage, Simon,' said Marcus suddenly, 'and it is one of which you should be proud.'

Simon hunched a shoulder and scowled.

'Papa took no interest in the farms,' he said. 'He always said we must do the job for which we were intended and leave others to know their own business.'

'And what,' asked Marcus Grant evenly, 'do you see as your own destiny — your *target* in life, if I might so word it?'

Simon reined in, an expression of bewilderment tempered with irritation on his good-looking face.

'I am not a farmer,' he protested. 'I am just a *gentleman*. Surely that is enough?'

Marcus sighed.

'As a gentleman with only slender means surely you should aim for better things for yourself and your family?' he suggested mildly enough.

Simon scowled blackly.

'I wish you would content yourself with spoiling my morning without adding to it by preaching me a sermon!' he said pettishly. 'Anyway — I thought saving my family from ruin was *your* affair, not mine!'

'A little co-operation and common civility would help greatly,' observed Marcus Grant with admirable restraint. 'It seems you are prepared to concede neither, Simon! Very well, I will be direct. The two farms upon the estate are being run at a loss. I intend that something should be done to improve matters. The smaller farm is run by a widow and her young son. Your father permitted them to stay after the farmer's death. They do their best and lack only guidance,' Marcus cast Simon a sidelong glance as the horses moved slowly onwards. He was heartened to see the lad's antagonism fade. Firmly he went on: 'The larger farm presents a problem.'

Simon frowned but seemed interested.

'Arkwright's farm?' he said. 'Yes, well what is wrong there?'

'It is *not* Arkwright's farm, at all!' pointed out Marcus shortly. 'Hazel Farm belongs to your family, Simon. Arkwright is merely your tenant! My investigations lead me to believe that Arkwright is both negligent and dishonest.'

Simon reined in, a look of unholy glee upon his face.

'Do you intend to cross swords with

Will Arkwright?' he grinned. 'I hope I may be there when you do so! He would be a bad man to cross. I'd advise you not to upset him!'

Marcus Grant refrained from comment, but turned his horse purposefully in the direction of Hazel Farm. For a moment Simon hesitated then, with a shrug, he followed. If Grant wanted to risk the length of Arkwright's tongue *and* the chance of being peppered with shot in the seat of his breeches, then he, Simon, would not deny himself the sight of this edifying spectacle!

* * *

It was mid-afternoon when Simon strode into Fortune Hall, having left his horse to the care of the stableman. Nicola followed him into the house, still wearing her 'working clothes' of breeches and shirt.

Mrs Fortune and Caroline were sitting upon a bench on the terrace, taking a well-earned rest after their labours with the roses and small Paula and David were playing with a kitten close beside them.

Simon marched out on to the terrace, closely followed by Nicola.

'Ah, so you are back, my love,' smiled Sophia Fortune. 'I trust you have spent a pleasant time with Mr Grant? I know that he is relying upon your help, dear.'

Simon wore a stunned look.

'You will not believe what your precious Grant has done *this* time, Mama,' he said. 'He made me go to Hazel Farm with him. He gave Will Arkwright an unvarnished opinion of his character and g — gave him notice to quit! Yes, Arkwright has but a week to pack up and go. I could scarcely take it all in but I have the strangest feeling that I stood my ground and backed up Grant! He's clever, is Marcus Grant, I'll give him that! He said he'd do nothing without my agreement and, in spite of myself, I found I was *agreeing* with him!'

'So that is that, my dear,' nodded his

mother comfortably. 'Well, I never did care for Will Arkwright. He treated his mother shamefully and I think she was quite glad to die, poor old soul!'

'I've never liked him either,' chimed in Nicola. 'He is a cruel man and even his own dog cringes away from him. Mr Grant has done the right thing!'

Caroline rose slowly to her feet.

'What is to become of Hazel Farm?' she asked quietly. 'Has the all-powerful Mr Grant made plans for its future?'

'He says,' said Simon darkly, 'that he has a suitable tenant ready and waiting to take possession. Before long we will find ourselves completely surrounded by the fellow's hirelings!'

His mother rose and looked him in the eyes.

'You will have a chance to question him later,' she said calmly. 'I have invited him here to dinner this evening.'

Nicola clasped her hands together with excited pleasure and begged immediately that she might be allowed to join the family. Being but fifteen, she usually found herself hovering between the nursery and adulthood and, on this occasion, she had no desire to be classed as a child along with David and Paula. She gave a gasp of relief when her mother smilingly agreed. Caroline ignored both this small exchange and her brother's noisy protests.

She stared unseeingly over the rose-bushes. The sight of Marcus Grant and Simon seated at the same dinner table would be enough on its own to rob her of all appetite, she thought wryly. Yet, that sight coupled with the knowledge of her mother's fond hopes for the future, could prove to be something of an ordeal. She found the prospect definitely daunting.

4

Sophia's roses were displayed in bowls and vases in both the dining-room and the drawing-room that evening and the furniture was so highly polished that the flowers were reflected in the woodwork. Someone had been working hard to show off the rooms at their best for this special occasion, thought Caroline.

During the last two years or so, the number of servants employed at the Hall had been drastically reduced and there were now fewer than was really necessary for the size of the place. Except for Bessie, who was both nursemaid and nursery-governess, as well as being general sewing-maid, there were only four indoor servants. Gregory the footman and Barnes the parlour-maid each had several additional duties to perform and Cook worked unaided except for the little kitchen-maid. Of what had once been a large outside staff, only Whitton remained to care for the horses and the kitchen-garden.

However, pondered Caroline wryly, it was highly likely that Marcus Grant considered them overstaffed! When one considered the financial position he was probably in the right to do so. She had never had the remotest idea of what was paid out in yearly wages to the staff, nor had it been her place to show interest in so mundane a matter. It would be fruitless to make enquiries on this score now that it had become Marcus Grant's province. At least, she thought with an attempt at humour, he had lightened the load by dismissing the Bassetts from the lodge! Perhaps they would be obliged to tighten their belts still further. Yet surely the remaining servants were each completely essential in their various ways? Trying to reassure herself that this must prove to be so, Caroline made her way to her own room.

Although Mr Fortune had died so

very recently, his widow had declared that full mourning dress must be discarded — especially for this evening. She was to wear grey and insisted that her daughters should put on their prettiest gowns.

'Caro! You have not even changed yet!' came Nicola's accusing voice at her bedroom door and Caroline started guiltily.

'No — I had best make haste,' she agreed with an attempt at gaiety. 'It will not do for me to keep our guardian waiting! Come in and let me see you, love!'

Nicola came into the room and pirouetted slowly for her sister's inspection. Her gown was of pale blue silk and was quite plain save for a decoration of small bows down the front and a frilling of lace at the elbow-length sleeves. Her fair curls were confined by a blue ribbon and her cheeks were pink with excitement.

'Nico, you look lovely and quite grown-up!' praised Caroline. 'No one would guess that this refined young lady was an urchin in breeches as recently as this very afternoon!'

Nicola chuckled then said soberly:

'I am sometimes glad that I am still young enough to be considered a child on occasions. Growing up brings responsibilities. I wish I could stay fifteen for ever more! I would be content to wear my breeches and care for the horses — knowing that I could always put on my best gown and become a young lady if I chose to do so!'

Caroline, who had been washing in tepid water at the bowl, picked up her gown from where it had been lying on the bed and asked her sister for help to put it on. She emerged from the folds of the gown, her hair untidily disarrayed and said with a smile:

'Well, I am five years your senior, love, and nothing dreadful or even *exciting* has happened to me with the passing of the years, so do not think time will change anything for you.'

She sat down on the dressing-stool

before her mirror and began to brush her curls into some semblance of order. Nicola fidgetted with a pincusion and looked across at her sister's reflection in the mirror.

'Things *are* different for you, Caro,' she said suddenly. '*I* have never had countless suitors at the door begging for my hand!'

'No more have I!' said Caroline lightly, setting down her brush with a clatter. 'And Papa's mode of exit from this earth has cut down what was only a small number, to a mere solitary one: dear, faithful Hubert!'

'Hubert? Oh, but he is *horrid*!' objected Nicola. She gave her sister a quick look and went on timidly: 'There is always Mr Grant. I think he is — '

'Then grow up fast, love, and have him for yourself!' said Caroline tautly, her colour high. 'Oh — you are just as bad as Mama!' She rose to her feet and smoothed down her skirts. 'Well — will I do, Nico?'

Nicola stepped back and scrutinised

her sister carefully.

'There is something — something *glowing* about you tonight,' she said breathlessly. 'You have not worn that gown before, have you?'

Caroline looked down at herself then smiled sadly.

'Papa chose it, love, not long before he died. Doubtless it was never paid for — but Mr Grant will have settled that account by now, I am sure.'

The gown was of dark blue figured silk and opened down the front to reveal a pale blue quilted petticoat decorated with frills. The sleeves were short to the elbow and the neckline was cut low and square. Caroline wore a single link of small, matched pearls about her throat and her hair was caught up higher than usual with one curl straying down on to her shoulder.

'Mr Grant will find us mere country-misses!' she warned Nicola. 'I am sure he is used to ladies with powdered hair and a deal more elegance than we will ever lay claim to!'

Surprisingly enough, dinner was something of a success, although Simon's mood seemed as black as the coat he had perversely decided on wearing. Sophia Fortune sat at the head of the table. On her insistence, the foot was left empty. She had Mr Grant upon her right and Caroline upon her left. Nicola was beside Mr Grant and Simon beside Caroline.

Caroline found she could not raise her eyes without looking fully into the dark ones of the guest and accepted ruefully that her mother had planned that this should happen.

Sophia, in her elegant grey gown, was an attentive hostess and, such was her skill that, before long, Simon had deigned to come out of the sulks a little and Nicola had recovered from the shyness which had resulted in finding herself next to Mr Grant at table.

The first course consisted of boiled neck of mutton, a chicken pie, soup and vegetables. Caroline took only soup and was therefore able to occupy herself with a discreet but thorough appraisal of the guest. Marcus Grant possessed the equal of Simon's vast appetite and, between the two of them, it seemed likely that the dishes would return to the kitchen completely empty.

Either from customary choice or from a desire not to overawe the Fortune family, Marcus wore his own hair, tied back simply with a black ribbon. In this age of wigs, only the serving-class and minor country gentlemen wore their own hair, but the style somehow suited Marcus. His brows and eyes were so dark that they seemed to demand a hair colour in keeping with their hue.

Gregory and Barnes removed the meagre remains of the first course and brought in the second. Caroline found she was now thinking of the servants as people and she noticed for the first time that grey was showing in Barnes' hair and that Gregory's shoulders had become stooped. Finding Marcus Grant's eyes upon her, she wondered if he could read her thoughts. Unthinkingly, she gave him a friendly smile — the first in their acquaintance. His eyes widened fractionally and he bowed his head slightly in acknowledgement of the proffered olive-branch, before giving his full attention to Mrs Fortune.

But it was *not* meant to be an olive-branch at all, thought Caroline crossly. She chose breast of veal with mushrooms from the second course and watched with growing incredulity as Marcus matched Simon in his inroad upon veal, fruit tarts and jellies with syllabub. She ended her own meal with an apple and continued her appraisal of the dinner-guest. He was so absorbed in his food and his hostess' conversation that Caroline felt she was safe to do so.

Although he did not wear a wig, there was nothing countrified about his dress. He wore a fashionable coat of dark green cloth with a high collar. His waistcoat was of embroidered satin and his shirt was ruffled at the front and at the wrists.

Up to now conversation had been upon general topics and had been mainly between Mrs Fortune and her guest. Simon had put in the odd remark and both Caroline and Nicola had responded when addressed directly.

'In a way, it is a pity that my father was unable to take up this guardianship-business,' said Marcus suddenly as he set down his napkin. His dark eyes were upon Caroline, although they flickered from time to time to Simon also. 'I think you would have found yourself better able to accept an older man. I had doubts at first on the sense of my accepting responsibility in this way. You must have wondered why I did so, instead of merely tendering my father's formal regrets. I shall not satisfy your curiosity on that point!' He smiled, but his tone was firm in the extreme. 'Your mother,' he nodded to Sophia, 'has decided that you must be put fully into the picture. Here are the facts! As individuals, you may each receive a small personal annual allowance — at your mother's discretion. As a family, I am pleased to tell you, you are now free of debt and are in a position to retain and *pay* the existing staff here. In the very near future, additional income will be made from the rent of the South Lodge, but it will not be used to supplement your personal allowances! There is much to be done here and I am determined to do my best for you. The tenant who will take over the lodge, is an old acquaintance of mine. He is a town tradesman,' Marcus paused and stared at Simon to discourage unfavourable comment. 'He is prepared to pay well for the privilege of renting a country retreat. He will not always be in residence but when he is there,' Marcus gave Simon another ponted look, 'he will be accorded courteous civility. He will not expect to ingratiate himself with you for your society is of a higher brand than that with which he is accustomed.' Marcus raised a dark brow at Simon's graceless snort then went on: 'The new tenant at Hazel Farm will pay an increased rent but Mrs Hardacre's rent for the smaller farm will be reduced — on condition that her son sets up a stall once weekly in the village to market produce.'

Once again Marcus Grant fell silent and this time his look of enquiry was directed at Caroline. The remark about marketing produce from a stall was more than her composure could take. It seemed only yesterday that she had declared that this activity might be expected of her!

'I — I am sorry, sir,' she managed. 'Pray continue.'

Marcus gave her a long look, then nodded.

'My next point may result in my being declared high-handed,' he began calmly. 'It concerns your nursemaid — and the children.'

An interruption occurred just then. Gregory entered, coughed apologetically and whispered urgently in Mrs Fortune's ear.

'Oh dear,' she said, rising resignedly.

'You must please excuse me. We have a crisis in the nursery! It is David. He is having nightmares again and naturally poor Bessie cannot cope alone.'

'Which is precisely my point,' said Marcus Grant under his breath. 'Come, I will go up to the nursery with you. I am reckoned to have a way with children.'

Left alone, the three younger Fortunes stared at each other in silence.

'He doesn't want to be thought high-handed!' choked Simon at length. 'The prosy bore! His place is in the lodge, doing our accounts. Mama had no right to bring him in here as an honoured guest.'

'We are not paying for his services, Simon,' said Caroline slowly, 'so who are we to dictate to *him*?'

'He looks very handsome in his green coat,' said Nicola with a dreamy sigh, 'and I am glad he does not wear a wig, for I dislike them!' In a more down-to-earth tone, she added: 'I will go up to the nursery to help with David.

He is often unmanagable after those horrid nightmares.'

Another minute elapsed and then Caroline announced her own intention of going up to the nursery. Simon raised his eyes heavenwards and said *he* had no desire to play nursemaid.

'I will be in the drawing-room when you decide to return,' he said, adding darkly that he had a mind to leave the house and go for a brisk ride. 'But I *won't*,' he muttered, 'or Mama will never let me hear the end of it!'

Nicola was standing in the nursery doorway and she put a finger to her lips when Caroline approached.

'He is over the worst, Caro,' she whispered. 'Mr Grant was right — he is marvellous with children!'

Several candles illuminated the nursery, casting madly dancing shadows from the draught from the open door. David was lying quietly back upon his pillows, his face white in the candlelight. In the other small bed, Paula slept on, heedless of both her brother's panicking screams and the unusual number of people present in the room.

Poor Bessie, the nursemaid, stood helplessly in the background and it was evident that Marcus alone had been the calming influence upon the child. He was still beside the bed and Caroline heard him say softly:

'Go to sleep now, David. You will not dream again. Remember you are to come to the lodge in the morning to see Quimby's pup!'

Try as she would, Caroline could not repress a quiver of shame. David's nightmares had had them all beaten for so long, yet Marcus Grant had found no difficulty in soothing the boy instantly.

When they were all in the drawing-room, Gregory brought in coffee and Mrs Fortune began to pour it carefully into the delicate china cups which had been part of her dowry.

Marcus took the cup she held out to him but made no attempt to drink from it. He stood with his back to the hearth, frowning impartially at the Fortune family.

'How long has this been going on?' he asked abruptly. 'A boy of ten should not have bad dreams. What is wrong with David?'

'He had a fall from a horse,' said Nicola, speaking quickly before anyone else could reply. She glanced round half-defiantly at her mother and went on: 'It happened about two years ago. I've always said he would have lost his fear if he'd been tossed straight back into the saddle! It was Papa's grey, you see, and David had no right to mount it. Papa saw him and shouted across the stableyard and — well, David fell off. He hit his leg on the mounting-block and has been lame ever since — ' She faltered into silence and went very pink, shaken by her own eloquence. 'It is best you know the story, Mr Grant,' she murmured.

'He was just a little boy of eight and he was badly hurt,' said his mother excusingly. 'How could we have lifted him back up on to that great brute's saddle? It would have been inhuman!'

Marcus Grant sighed.

'I was about to speak of the children when we were interrupted,' he said slowly. 'Bessie is probably a good nursemaid but she is not suited to have the children in her sole care, day and night. David should have a tutor — or go away to school. Even Paula is not too young to begin a proper timetable of lessons. Also, Nicola is rather young to have bidden a complete farewell to the schoolroom.'

Nicola's affronted scowl made her look so like Simon, that Caroline found difficulty in restraining a smile.

'David is not strong enough to stand the hurly-burly life of school and tutors cost money,' said Sophia flatly. 'Marcus, you insist that we practise economy and now you suggest that we pay yet another servant!'

'The person I have in mind would scarcely deign to class herself as a servant,' said Marcus with a grin which took years from his age. 'Now, listen please, before you refuse me out of hand! Miss Patchett was once governess to my sisters and also to me. She is still living in my family home and grumbles incessantly that she must remain idle. If she agreed to come and teach David and Paula — yes, and Nicola also, for a year at least — then she would expect no payment except board and lodging. Consider too, it can scarcely aid young David's self-respect to be taught by his small sister's nursemaid. Sharing lessons with a governess would be another matter entirely! I am quite sure that Bessie would be pleased to have her duties halved,' he finished calmly.

Little more was said on the subject and Marcus Grant had his way. As it was now quite late he thanked Sophia for the evening and bade the family good-night, then prepared to leave.

'Do not forget to send David down to the lodge to see Quimby's pup,' he added, then made his exit.

5

The following week proved to be an eventful one. It began with Marcus Grant attending Sunday service in the village church with the Fortune family, for the first time. It ended with the arrival of Miss Honoria Patchett, the governess.

Finding Caroline strangely subdued when he railed on at the impertinence of Grant's coming to church with them, Simon aired his grievance instead before the willing ear of his friend, Cedric Channing.

Cedric, a thin dark supercilious youth of nineteen, was brother to Caroline's admirer, Hubert. Their father, Sir Luke Channing, owned the estate which neighboured the Fortune property.

'Just because Grant holds our purse-strings, he thinks we must all bow down before him!' grated Simon angrily.

'Mama has just informed me that I am to receive an allowance of a few paltry shillings a week. It is all Grant's doing! He insists he is doing his best for us but I am sure he is revelling in this situation!'

'Well — if he is as well-heeled himself as he appears, it might be a good idea if you could get him to wed one of your sisters — then you would *all* profit!' suggested Cedric practically. Proof of the little love lost between him and his brother, Hubert, showed when he added: 'How about marrying him off to Caroline? That would be one in the eye for Hubert!'

'Caro detests the fellow,' said Simon. 'Nico likes him well enough but she is a mere schoolroom chit! No you'll have to think up a better plan than that, old man! Anyway, I would hate to think we had *him* with us forever!'

The Channings were a far from wealthy family and Cedric's own allowance scarcely exceeded that of Simon. Indeed, in the better times of perhaps two years ago, it had been Simon who had played his friend's banker for trifling amounts.

'We both need money,' said the dark youth, giving his friend a sidelong look, 'and there are ways and means of getting it — if you have the courage! It is not a game for fainthearts, though! I've spoken of this before, Simon, so you know perfectly well what I am talking about!'

Simon shuffled his feet uncomfortably.

'It's too dangerous by half, Cedric,' he muttered, 'and, if things went wrong, it would *kill* Mama. No — that game is not for me!'

'Think of an alternative?' asked Cedric carelessly. 'Well — keep it in mind, Simon, and we'll speak of it again.'

Simon made excuses for being unable to stay longer at the Channings home. Disconsolately he rode back to the Hall, only to mutter blackly to himself when he discovered Marcus Grant's brown mare in the stall next to his.

'Damned liberty-taker!' he gritted bad-temperedly to the stableman.

'Mrs Fortune said Mr Grant was to use t'stable, Mr Simon, sir,' said Whitton placidly. He was a grizzled man in his early sixties and did not stand in awe of Simon, whom he had known from childhood. 'Reckon you'd not expect him to tie up his poor mare to t'lodge door-post, like?'

Simon did not deign to answer and stamped off moodily into the house. Thoroughly out of patience with life, he wondered fleetingly if perhaps he should pay heed to Cedric Channing's outrageous idea. Somehow it did not appeal to him, even in his present mood of rebellion.

Seeking a sympathetic ear, he wandered about the house and finally found his mother, Caroline and Nicola, together with Bessie and the children, working diligently beyond the terrace. The nursemaid and her charges were tugging out the tufts of grass which marred the drive. Sophia and her elder daughters were attempting to prune back the evergreen bushes which flanked the Hall-end of the drive.

Simon stared at his family in stunned horror.

'Why not get Whitton and that fellow Quimby to hack off a foot or so at each side of the drive?' he asked at last. 'Mama — what has come over you? This is not work for a lady!'

His mother, flushed with exertion, shook her head.

'Hacking would give an untidy raw look,' she explained. 'We are merely clipping off the branches which grow out over the drive. Can you not see an improvement already, my love? The roses on the terrace are a *picture* now — exactly as they were when you were David's age. Soon we will have everything in order again!'

Simon stared uncomprehendingly.

'Why, Mama?' he said. 'It's that Grant fellow, is it not? How like him to make *ladies* slave like peasants!'

'If you are going to be horrid, Simon, then do go away and be horrid somewhere else!' urged Nicola. 'We were getting along *famously* before you arrived with your long face and your grumbles. Of *course* Mr Grant did not tell us to work in the grounds. He is doing *his* part and we are doing *ours*! In case you had not noticed, my big brother, this is a reformed family and soon we will have won back our self-respect!'

'Bravo, Nico, love!' smiled her mother. 'Yes, Simon — we have decided to smarten up the grounds. Being our own labourers certainly cuts down the cost!'

Caroline smiled at Simon's genuine amazement.

'I think you have all gone mad,' he said flatly. 'Scrubbing about with a pair of hand-shears and a trowel would do nothing to boost *my* self respect.' He rounded on his elder sister who was openly laughing and said cuttingly: 'You'll never get a husband, Caro! If

Hubert Channing could see you now, with mud on your cheek and rent in your skirt — even *he* would stay away!'

Caroline paled with shock. Simon had never before spoken so unkindly to her and there had been real venom in his tone. She opened her mouth to speak but was forestalled.

'I am about to take my guardian's duties seriously,' came the chilly tones of Marcus Grant. 'You will apologize instantly to your sister, you graceless pup, and consider this week's allowance cut!' Simon went white and moved as if to strike out at Grant. 'Try *that*, my fine stripling, and it will be the last move you make,' said the older man harshly. 'Now, make your apology to Caroline and get out of my sight!'

Simon's hands clenched into fists and he thrust out his jaw.

'I *am* sorry, Caroline,' he said in a low, quivering voice. 'You know I did not mean to hurt you.' He spun round and faced the granite-faced Marcus Grant. 'I would have craved pardon of

Caro, anyway,' he spat out, 'so don't crow about your victory! You have not heard the last of this, Grant! I may be under age and subject to your petty punishments, but one day you'll pay for your damned interference!'

Sophia Fortune stepped forward, her breast heaving, but Marcus Grant put a hand on her arm as Simon stalked off.

'Let him go,' he advised. 'Give him time to cool off. Unless he learns to curb that unruly temper, young Simon is going to clash head-on with the world in general. Now — I meant what I said about this week's allowance so do not undermine my authority by slipping a few shillings into his pocket, any of you!' He smiled but his tone was firm. Then he relaxed and turned to the silent younger members of the family. 'I suggest you all go indoors now and take luncheon. You must not over-do the hard labour. Your work does you credit!'

'Thank you Mr Grant,' beamed Nicola. 'We have decided to do our best for you.' She blushed a fiery red and added quickly: 'And for *ourselves*, of course! We really have been lax about things but we have turned over a new leaf, we promise you!'

Marcus Grant chuckled and the family turned to go indoors.

'Caroline,' he said suddenly, 'would you spare me another moment, please?'

She hesitated on the threshold, her colour rising at his use of her first name. Nicola looked back too then, unwillingly, followed her mother.

'It is my presence here that has caused this change in your brother,' said Marcus without preamble. 'Simon resents me at every turn and blames me for the feeling of unrest within himself. I suppose it is only natural but I suspect his life has been far too easy up to now! Was he ever whipped for insolence as a schoolboy, I wonder? I must confess to having the impulse to thrash him thoroughly and personally!' He paused and looked down at her thoughtfully. 'Should I leave, Caroline? Come, let me have your honest opinion.

Perhaps I have been a trifle cold-blooded in my approach to your family problems. You see — there is a frighteningly small amount of capital. Only by bringing in extra rents and practising severe economy, can I hope to achieve your survival. It is as serious as *that*!'

'Survival?' echoed Caroline. 'I have heard Mama use that word, too! We none of us realised how bad the position is, you see.' She took a deep breath and gazed up at him, her eyes very blue. 'Please stay, Mr Grant,' she begged. 'Without you, *survival* will be impossible. Pay no heed to Simon. He is only a boy and can do nothing, for all his talk!'

If she felt a twinge of disloyalty for belittling her brother in this way, she squashed it resolutely. Larger issues were at stake than Simon's sense of importance! Suddenly she looked down in bewilderment. Mr Grant had possessed himself of her hand.

'We will make a new beginning, my

dear,' he said with a smile and raised her hand to his lips.

Somewhat bemusedly, Caroline made her way indoors, thinking not of the problem of Simon but of this new slant upon the character of Marcus Grant. Suddenly she pressed the hand he had kissed to her cheek.

'Romantic *idiot*!' she admonished herself a second later and went to the dining-room in search of refreshment.

* * *

On Friday afternoon a coach and four arrived at the main door of Fortune Hall. Gregory received the passenger, a cord-bound trunk, numerous boxes and packages and a small pug dog.

'Kindly inform your mistress that Miss Patchett has come!' ordered the new governess in a loud booming tone, which contrasted sharply with her small stature and mild brown eyes.

'Er — yes, ma'am,' agreed Gregory, eyeing the dog askance.

It put its head on one side and stared back at him from round, protruding eyes, with an odd unfocussed look.

Left in the entrance hall with her pet and her baggage, Honoria Patchett pursed her lips and allowed her eyes to make a full tour of inspection of her immediate surroundings. She saw a wide, gracious, carpeted stairway, dark undistinguished-looking oil paintings of dead and gone Fortunes and a huge bowl of roses upon a side table.

'Miss Patchett?' enquired a voice from the stairs and Caroline descended with a smile. 'Mama is resting and you will meet her presently. It is all right, Gregory,' she said, dismissing the manservant. 'I will show Miss Patchett to her room.'

Honoria Patchett held out her hand in greeting.

'You must be Miss Caroline,' she said gruffly. 'Mr Mark said you were a beauty. Now don't mind Jacob! He goes everywhere with me and is a perfect gentleman. He will need a basket in my room and I will discuss his diet with your cook later.'

Caroline's eyes were brimful with surprised amusement, but she took the proffered hand and nodded gravely to the goggle-eyed Jacob. They ascended the stairs side by side and when Caroline halted at a door, she turned and said:

'Bessie is to keep her room next to the nursery. Mama thought you would wish to be more private.' She opened the door and stood aside for the governess to enter. 'You are next to my sister, Nicola, and you have a view of the roses on the terrace. I hope you will be happy with us! Mr Grant has decided that the children are in sad need of proper tuition and discipline.'

Miss Patchett crossed to the window and looked down appreciatively at the roses, Jacob snuffling at her heels. Then she turned to look at Caroline.

'We shall do very well here, Jacob and I,' she said in her loud, clear voice. 'I was becoming bored at High Crags.

There has been little for me to do since Miss Sarah left the schoolroom, you see.'

'Sarah? Is she Mr Grant's sister?' asked Caroline curiously.

Honoria Patchett nodded.

'Yes. He has two sisters. The elder one was married some time ago. She is now Mrs James Ratcliffe. Miss Sarah is nineteen and still at home.'

'Mr Grant has told us nothing at all about himself and his family,' admitted Caroline quietly, 'but, then, he was not very well received here. I am afraid that we were ready to resent a guardian when we heard the terms of Papa's will.'

The governess gave her a long unsmiling look.

'Mr Mark's father's health is only fair,' she said rebukingly. 'We did not expect that Mr Mark should take your family's cares upon his shoulders. He is by far too young for you to regard him in the light of a father-substitute.'

Caroline gave a sudden choke of laughter.

'I do assure you that we have come to rely upon him greatly,' she said, 'but I hope I must not begin to call him Papa!'

Honoria Patchett shook her head chidingly, but smiled nevertheless. At this point, Gregory and Barnes knocked at the open door.

'Your baggage, ma'am,' said Gregory, raising an eyebrow at the little dog which had trotted towards him and was fixing him with an unwinking stare.

'If you would like to come to the nursery and meet the children, Barnes will unpack in your absence,' suggested Caroline. 'Please bring Jacob. David will be delighted that you have a dog. He has made a friend of a pup Quimby keeps at the lodge, but it is young and untrained and Mama will not have it in the house.'

They left the bedroom with Jacob padding along in their wake and ascended a further flight of stairs. The nursery-quarters consisted of one small and two large, adjoining rooms. The small room was Bessie's and the children slept in the centre one.

‘Ah, so this is the schoolroom is it?’ boomed Miss Patchett in a tone of satisfaction.

From that day no one ever again referred to the ‘nursery’. It was now the schoolroom and even small Paula was elevated to the status of scholar. When they entered, Paula was drawing squeakily upon her slate and David was sitting writing at the long, ink-stained table. Bessie, who had been sewing beside the window, rose quickly and bobbed a curtsey. She was plump and placid and past first youth. Such was her nature that it did not occur to her to resent the arrival of the governess. The children’s education would now be the newcomer’s responsibility, but Bessie’s position in the household was unchanged. She would still put the children to bed at night, admit their mother to hear their prayers, then keep a loving ear upon them till they slept. She would still wake them in the morning and serve them breakfast at the small table by their bedroom window. She would still sew and mend the family's clothing and keep an eye upon the state of the linen. Yes, Bessie's position was assured. She would be too fully occupied to complain at the manner in which her load had lightened.

The children rose to their feet and rushed over to greet Caroline with boisterous hugs, while Miss Patchett stood by, her face expressionless. Caroline turned, an arm about each child, her blue eyes pleading that the governess' first remark should not be a rebuke to her young charges.

'How do you do, David and Paula?' boomed Honoria Patchett, holding out a hand to each of them in turn. 'I am Miss Patchett! Come, bring your books to the table and let me see how far advanced you are in your studies, children.'

'M — may the little dog stay?' asked David shyly.

'He never leaves me,' said Miss Patchett. 'Come, Jacob, shake hands and be friends!'

The small pug obediently held out a forepaw to the delighted children. Over their heads, Miss Patchett gave a smile and a nod. Knowing she had received her dismissal, Caroline moved to the door, seeing Bessie gather up her work and head for the next room. Miss Patchett's reign had begun!

Barnes had just finished the governess's unpacking when Caroline descended the schoolroom stairs.

'Would you take Miss Patchett a tea-tray, Barnes?' she asked. 'She has plunged straight into her duties. Perhaps the little dog would like a bowl of milk or water also.'

Caroline next went out to the stableyard to inform her sister that the governess had arrived. Nicola, clad in her breeches and an outgrown shirt of Simon's, grimaced.

'I suppose I must change into a gown before I go up to introduce myself!' she said wryly.

Caroline laughed.

'If you greet Miss Patchett in *that*

attire, Nico, she will put you nicely in your place!' she said. 'She is only small but she has a very loud voice and a *very* firm manner. I am glad I am old enough to be out of her reach!'

However, when the schoolroom routine was established, Nicola found no cause for complaint. She was to report to Miss Patchett after breakfast each day and was free by the luncheon-hour. David and Paula were to receive further tuition after luncheon also, but this was to include a walk out of doors with Jacob and his mistress, when weather permitted. As Mrs Fortune was pleased to remark to Marcus Grant after the end of the governess' first week:

'Miss Patchett is invaluable! I do not know how we ever went on before she joined us!'

6

After what he termed his 'humiliation' at the hands of the family guardian, Simon carefully avoided Marcus Grant's company. Indeed, for the greater part of each day he was absent from home, leaving after breakfast and only returning when evening came.

'Simon spends too much time with that sly Channing boy,' Mrs Fortune confided fretfully to Caroline. 'I cannot like Cedric, even though he is our neighbour's child. He is not the right sort of friend for Simon. I wonder what mischief those two boys can be hatching?'

'Do not worry so, Mama,' advised Caroline. 'You know how Simon behaves when he is in one of his moods! He is still sulking at Marcus Grant's reprimand.'

Sophia shook her head doubtfully.

'I cannot help but wonder if Marcus did the right thing when he withheld Simon's allowance last week. Simon is at a difficult age, my love! He is no longer a child, nor yet is he fully adult. I wish he would concern himself more with his home and his estate! After all, they will be his before very long. Marcus will not always be here to help and guide us. I shudder to think what my foolish Simon will do once the reins are in *his* hands.'

'Mama — I am sure you need not be anxious,' consoled Caroline. 'Perhaps Simon is wise to stay clear of Mr Grant for a time. We do not wish for another horrid incident like the last one, now do we?'

Simon was last at table that evening. With barely concealed malice he glanced round at his mother and sisters.

'Arkwright quit Hazel Farm yesterday,' he said, '*but* he intends to stay on in the district and he has become extremely *thick* with Bassett!'

He began to eat his meal and Mrs

Fortune exchanged a frown with her daughters.

'I think you should explain further, Simon,' said Caroline quietly. 'Exactly *what* do you mean?'

Simon grinned.

'I told you that Will Arkwright wouldn't take his marching orders with a good grace!' he said. 'Bassett's an idle, lumpish fellow but, partnered by Arkwright — who knows what will happen now? Grant evicted them both so he must bear the consequences! I would not be in *his* shoes, at any price!'

'Now this is foolish talk, love,' said his mother faintly. 'You cannot mean to suggest that Marcus could come to actual harm at the hands of these men? Why — Marcus has full authority to deal with the estate. He may employ and dismiss as he thinks fit. It is his privilege!'

Simon gave a less than pleasant smile.

'I'll say no more,' he said irritatingly. 'Ah, rabbit pie, Gregory! Do bring it over here, for I'm vastly hungry!'

Nicola stared with distaste at her brother, then scowled.

'You've *changed*, Simon!' she said. 'I do not even think I like you any more. If Miss Patchett hears you threatening Mr Grant's safety, there will be trouble! You only brought up the subject because she is not eating with us tonight!'

The governess had been invited to join the family for meals, but sometimes begged to be excused. Tonight, she was eating from a tray in her room and preparing her schoolroom work as she ate. She was a very conscientious teacher and had high hopes of David's scholastic ability. Nicola and small Paula just did not *care*, she mourned, but David had the makings of a scholar. As Nicola had observed just now at table, Marcus Grant's old governess would not take kindly to Simon's cheerful prognostications of the fate of her former pupil.

'Old Hatchett?' scoffed Simon rudely. 'What has she to say to anything? Why should I worry about an elderly governess and her wheezy little pug?'

His mother rose to her feet, gripped the edge of the table for support and said in a remarkably steady tone:

'I have had a full sufficiency of your mannerless behaviour, Simon! Pray leave the room this *instant*!'

For a moment her son froze, then he grinned and tossed down his knife and fork.

'Who cares for rabbit pie, anyway?' he enquired. He flicked his eyes round his silent family and his smile vanished. 'Treat me as a disobedient child, if you must, but soon you will see your error! I intend to show the lot of you *exactly* what I am capable of! Dear, naughty Simon has just come to a major decision!'

He made a lordly exit, shutting the door sharply behind him.

'I think,' said Sophia Fortune in failing tones, 'that I am about to suffer a *spasm*!'

'Oh, no you are *not*, Mama!' said Caroline hastily. 'Now, take a deep breath and steady yourself! Simon is not worth your distress.'

'Come, Mama!' rallied Nicola, rising to her feet and going to put an arm about her mother's shoulders. 'Do not go back into your old ways! You have been a different person since Mr Grant arrived!'

'And so,' said Mrs Fortune wearily, 'has Simon! Perhaps, after all, it would have been better if Marcus had never come. We might not have feared too badly with Great-Aunt Martha, you know!'

* * *

Despite the good advice of her daughters, Mrs Fortune found she could not lightly dismiss Simon's mood of insolent threats. She spent much of the following day lying upon the couch in her bedroom, with the curtains drawn against the summer sunshine and her smelling-bottle at the ready.

Gregory, coming in search of his

mistress to announce the arrival of two complete strangers, met a firm refusal from Barnes.

'You can't disturb Madam now,' protested the elderly maid. 'She's not well and is resting.'

Gregory frowned helplessly.

'There's this Mr and Mrs Brown waiting to see her,' he explained. 'They are the tenants Mr Grant got for the South Lodge. What am I to do with them, if I can't have a word with Madam?'

Barnes frowned back at him.

'If Mr Grant's taken it on himself to let the lodge, then it's his place to greet the tenants,' she said sharply. 'We'll not disturb the poor mistress. Happen Miss Caroline will know what to do.'

Gregory shook his head gloomily. He went back down the stairs to where he had left the callers. The library door stood ajar, so he tapped before entering and was relieved to find that Caroline had already discovered Mr and Mrs Brown. She turned to the manservant, her eyes puzzled.

'Gregory,' she said. 'Mr Brown tells me that Marcus Grant was to meet them at the South Lodge, but he is nowhere to be found. Mr Brown has dismissed his hired coach and left his baggage upon the lodge doorstep.'

'Aye, I reckon t'door's locked, miss,' agreed the new tenant, a stocky, shrewd-eyed Yorkshireman with a no-nonsense air about him. 'Mr Grant said as how he'd be waiting to show us in and get us settled, like, but we can't find him. I left Mabel — Mrs Brown, that is — to keep an eye on t'baggage and I walked round to t'West Lodge. Happen there's nobody there either — but for a dog barking fit to bust, inside.'

'We'd not have troubled *you*, Miss Fortune, if we could have found Mr Grant,' apologised his wife, a rosy-cheeked little woman in an outmoded gown.

Caroline exchanged a helpless look with Gregory.

'I wonder where Mr Grant's man,

Quimby, can be?' she murmured. 'Perhaps he and his master were called away. It seems rather odd and unlike Mr Grant. He should have been there to receive you. However, Gregory will bring you some refreshment. You must be quite ready for something, after your journey. Coach-riding can be tedious!'

'Eh — Miss Fortune, I could just do wi' a nice hot cup o' tea!' admitted Mabel Brown. 'If it's not too much trouble?' she added timidly.

Caroline smiled.

'A cup of tea is the very least we can offer, in the circumstances!' she said. 'Now, if you will excuse me, I will go in search of another key to the South Lodge. I am sure one must exist. Perhaps Whitton, our stableman, will know.'

She went up to her mother's room first and entered quietly.

'Oh, it is you, Caroline!' said Sophia, sleepily raising her head from a cushion. 'What is amiss, my dear?'

Caroline sat down on the edge of the

couch and spread her hands ruefully.

'The Browns have arrived,' she announced.

'Browns?' said her mother blankly. 'I do not recall having met anyone of that name.'

'Nor have you yet, love!' said Caroline with a smile. 'They are the tenants for the South Lodge.'

'Oh,' said her mother comfortably, 'well, Marcus will see to them. Letting the lodge was his idea. He must deal with these Browns. It is not really up to *me* to do anything.'

Caroline frowned thoughtfully.

'Apparently he agreed to greet their arrival,' she explained. 'But he is nowhere to be found and the lodge is locked. I wondered if there might be another key so that the Browns could let themselves in.'

Mrs Fortune gave the matter a moment's thought, then shook her head.

'I believe Marcus had a new lock fitted,' she said, 'so he will have all the keys himself. Now, where can he be? It is not like him to be late when he has made an arrangement. You must ask Quimby for the key, love. I am surprised you did not think of that for yourself!'

'Quimby is not at home,' explained Caroline patiently. 'It seems that his pup is the only occupant of the West Lodge. When Mr Brown knocked, the pup began to bark,' she smiled and added: 'He is barking 'fit to bust', according to our new tenant.'

Sophia Fortune prepared unwillingly to get up from the couch.

'You must give me a few moments to tidy my hair, love,' she said resignedly. 'I suppose I must come down to meet your Browns. It is too bad of Marcus, not to be awaiting their arrival!'

Caroline smiled ruefully to herself. Poor Marcus Grant, she thought. He did not have to transgress far to fall from her mother's favour!

Time went by and the new tenants grew more and more uncomfortable at being obliged to impose themselves upon the Fortune family. Caroline and Whitton and Nicola had searched fruitlessly for Grant and his manservant. Marcus' horse was not in her customary stall in the stables, so it seemed safe to assume that he was out riding, but it seemed odd that Quimby, too, should be absent. When the children were released from the schoolroom and David learned that Quimby's pup was now howling unconsolably in the locked West Lodge, he begged that something be done. Eventually it was decided that Whitton should break a kitchen window, so that David could climb in to comfort the pup.

Once the boy had made sure that the animal was merely lonely and not in any way hurt, he unbolted the kitchen door to admit Whitton and his sisters. A brief search proved the lodge to be unoccupied and Caroline let out her breath in a relieved sigh. It had suddenly occurred to her that Marcus and his manservant might possibly have been lying helpless in their beds, overcome by some violent illness.

To the unpracticed eyes of the Fortune sisters, there was no clue as to what might be amiss. However, Whitton felt confident in making an assumption.

'I'd say as how Quimby has gone away for t'day,' he said. 'See — there's a cold meal ready under covers on t'dining table. Quimby's prepared his master's dinner and gone somewhere. There's naught to worry about, young ladies. Happen Mr Grant's been delayed. He'll be back soon, I don't doubt.'

'Quimby would not have left poor little Soppy without food,' pointed out David. 'He must have *thought* Mr Grant wouldn't be long.'

Seeing the child's lip beginning to tremble, Caroline tried to ignore her own nagging anxiety. She put an arm about David's shoulders.

'Soppy?' she said. 'What a singular name for a pup!'

'He's Blenkinsop really,' explained David, 'but Quimby says he'll have to *grow* to such a long name. Soppy will do till he's trained.'

There was little that they could do at the West Lodge, so they went back up to the Hall, taking Soppy with them. Whitton stayed behind to await Mr Grant's arrival.

'I'll fill in t'time by boarding-up the broken window,' he said gruffly.

There seemed but one alternative to breaking-in also to the South Lodge to admit the Browns. With a sigh, Sophia Fortune invited her new tenants to dinner.

'Eh, my lady — I mean madam,' began Mabel Brown in a flustered tone. 'It wouldn't *do*, I'm sure!'

Her husband quelled her with a look.

'We'd be grateful to accept, Mrs Fortune,' he said simply, 'but don't go thinking we'll be planning to make a habit of it. We're simple folk, Mabel and I and we know our place. Yon South Lodge will suit us a treat, *when* young Grant decides to let us in!' he added, his eyes twinkling.

When Simon arrived home, he exclaimed bitterly at being obliged to eat with the tenants but, fortunately, only grumbled in his mother's private ear.

They were halfway through the second course, when Quimby arrived. Making a brief apology, he asked if he might have a word with Mrs Fortune. Seeing the look in his eyes and noting the way in which a nerve twitched in his cheek, Sophia set down her napkin and left the room with him.

'What's wrong with the fellow?' asked Simon carelessly, quirking up an eyebrow. 'I've never known Mama to leave the table before dinner is over. Ah, well — *everything* is a little odd and out of place today!'

Mr Brown's shrewd eyes turned to Simon.

'If you're referring to me an' Mabel, young sir,' he said calmly, 'then save your breath! Your lady mother kindly offered us dinner and, rather than keep my poor Mabel standing waiting on t'lodge doorstep, I agreed. It's not an occasion to be repeated, rely on that!'

Simon was somewhat taken aback by the man's blunt, forthright and by no means subservient manner and he was moved to mutter a grudging apology.

Mrs Fortune came back into the room with a very worried expression on her face and her daughters were quick to beg knowledge of the situation.

'Quimby has just arrived back from an errand to High Crags, Marcus' home,' she said frowningly. 'Apparently Marcus intended merely to ride round the estate and arrive back in good time to greet the arrival of Mr and Mrs Brown. However, he has *still* not returned and Quimby intends to set up a search-party. I believe he thinks Marcus might have met with an accident.'

'Well — one thing is for sure,' said Nicola. 'He will not have taken a tumble from his horse! He is a marvel in the saddle. Oh, mama! May I put on my breeches and join in the search?

Please say that I may!'

'Certainly not, my love!' said her mother in horror. 'Why — it is becoming quite dark. No — only the men must go and they must take lanterns.'

Mr Brown rose ponderously to his feet.

'I'll be pleased to help, if you can lend me a horse, ma'am,' he offered. 'T'more of us there are, t'more ground we'll cover!'

Caroline looked at Simon, waiting for him to forget his antipathy for Marcus and offer his help in turn. Instead, he kept his eyes upon his plate and gave no comment. She wondered a little at her brother's determination to have nothing to do with the family guardian, even under these new circumstances, but quickly forgot her puzzlement in the general clamour of suggestions and advice.

Quimby, Whitton, Gregory and Mr Brown set out into the dusk with lanterns; Simon disappeared from the room without saying where he was going and the ladies were left to wait and conjecture. Nicola seethed helplessly at being constrained to stay at home and Caroline bit worriedly upon her lip, pondering on Marcus Grant's possible fate.

It was late when the search-party returned. Only Mr Brown came indoors to greet the waiting ladies. Mutely he held out a bunch of keys to his wife.

'We'd best be off to yon South Lodge, Mabel, love,' he said heavily. 'Quimby found us t'keys.' Slowly he turned to face Sophia Fortune, her daughters and Miss Patchett, the governess, who had joined the party awaiting news. 'Reckon we were right,' he said. 'Young Mr Grant's been injured! We found him lying up on t'moors — beyond some farm or other, according to Quimby. His horse had stayed beside him where he fell. We saw t'horse first then went up close and found *him* lying on his face in t'bracken.'

Caroline went very pale and rose

unsteadily to her feet.

'Then he *did* fall from his horse!' she said. 'Is — is he badly hurt?'

Mr Brown frowned bodingly.

'Nay — happen this was no ordinary riding-accident,' he said sombrely. 'I'd say as how someone had a grudge against young Grant. He'd been *shot*, see, an' left for dead!'

7

Marcus Grant's injury proved to be not too serious after all, but he had lost a good deal of blood from being left so long untended upon the moor. Quimby was very firm in banning visitors from his master's sickroom.

'He must have complete rest, madam,' said the manservant, immovably polite, when Mrs Fortune arrived at the West Lodge armed with her condolences and a huge bunch of roses. 'You may see him when he is a little stronger.'

Strangely enough, young David found no difficulty in gaining access to Marcus' room. When questioned by his curious sisters, the boy only smiled and said simply:

'I do not *worry* him, you see. I sit quietly by his bed and speak only if he addresses me. He says I am to come whenever I wish!'

The less favoured members of the family could do little save await Marcus Grant's return to full health. At least they were consoled with the knowledge that he hoped he would soon be well.

One afternoon, Hubert Channing paid an unexpected call upon the Fortunes. Of slight build and less than average height, he bore a striking resemblance to his younger brother, Cedric. Before her father's death, Caroline had regarded Hubert in the indulgently careless light of one of many suitors. She had never favoured him above the rest and had wondered why he alone should remain constant when the scandal of Papa's untimely end had driven away the others.

Seated in the drawing-room on the afternoon of his visit, Caroline eyed him critically, giving a mental frown for his elaborate wig, the obvious padding in the shoulders of his coat and his somewhat affected mode of speech. She found she was comparing him unfavourably with Marcus Grant and pondered irritably on why he had chosen to visit them today. Her thoughts and her concern were all for the injured Marcus and she resented Hubert's intrusion with a ferocity which astonished even herself. She started visibly when Hubert ended his dissertation upon the weather and the health of his parents and spoke suddenly of Marcus.

'It was odd, was it not, this incident which involved that agent-fellow, Grant,' he observed. 'We heard that he had been shot and wondered if the highwayman might be the culprit!'

'*Highwayman*?' echoed Sophia Fortune faintly. 'Oh, no — never say there is a highwayman in the district!'

Hubert nodded his bewigged head gravely.

'Oh, it is true enough, ma'am,' he said. 'The Marriotts' coach was held up only last week and Mr Marriott was relieved of his purse.'

'I do not think that a highwayman

could be responsible for the attack upon Mr Grant,' put in Caroline shortly. 'As far as we are aware, poor Mr Grant was shot in broad daylight. Surely highwaymen prowl only at night?'

'Well, depend upon it,' began Hubert, 'this must have been a case of mistaken identity! No one but a fool would expect a mere *agent* to be worth robbing!'

Caroline rose sharply to her feet and crossed to stand beside the window.

'Marcus Grant is a gentleman,' she said across her shoulder. 'Although he is helping us to manage our affairs, he is no paid employee! If robbery were indeed the object, then I have no doubt he stood to lose far more than Mr Marriott!'

Hubert, who had politely risen when she did so, narrowed his eyes at the vehemence of her words.

'I beg pardon, Caroline,' he said, his tone patently insincere. 'I had no idea that you held the fellow in esteem.'

For an instant, she stared back at him, then she said unsteadily:

'You must excuse me, Mama — Hubert. I am afraid I have a headache!'

She was out of the room before the visitor could note the prick of tears at her eyes and the break in her voice. Marcus had been their good friend and had been injured while going about his self-imposed duties. She could not bear to hear that odious Hubert Channing pour scorn upon him.

Once in her own room, she quickly composed herself, annoyed that she should have let Hubert disturb her so easily. She found she was pondering on his revelation about the activity of a highwayman in the district. It was probably nothing but an invention of Hubert's young brother, the sly, mischievous Cedric, she decided. Highway robbery was a major offence and punishable by death. It was some time since their local roads had been plagued by a thief of this kind, in fact, Caroline had been a mere child when the self-styled Captain Swift had been gibbetted in chains at the crossroads. She shuddered now at the fleeting memory of a blackened, tarred corpse swinging in the breeze. Surely it would be a very hardy highwayman who would risk the ultimate penalty on the chance of taking the half-empty purses of the impoverished local people? No — Hubert had been misled by that brother of his! If Mr Marriott *had* lost his purse, it was highly likely that that gentleman had been too intoxicated to note the manner of its going!

Caroline quickly became irked by the four walls of her room and pondered on where to go without being obliged to speak again to Hubert Channing. On impulse, she went up to the schoolroom. Although Miss Patchett was firm mistress of her own domain, lessons must almost be at an end and conversation with the forthright governess would be decidedly preferrable to solitary seclusion until Hubert departed! She rapped politely upon the schoolroom door before entering. The small pug, Jacob, came to sniff at her heels and she bent to pat his smooth, cream-coloured head.

'Do come in, Miss Caroline!' boomed Honoria Patchett. 'We are about to set off upon our daily walk with Jacob. I hope that you will join us. It is a fine, sunny day but we intend to keep to the paths, because of yesterday's rain.'

The little dog stared up, goggle-eyed, at Caroline as if to add his own persuasion and she gave a sudden nod.

'Yes,' she said, with a smile for David and Paula. 'I believe a breath of fresh air is what I am lacking. We have a visitor, you see, and I am afraid that his talk has given me a headache.'

Her young brother put a sympathetic hand upon hers.

'Yes, come and walk with us, Caro!' he urged. 'Headaches are horrid! It must be Hubert Channing who has come. No one else could give you a headache just by *talking*!'

'David is always right!' said Caroline

lightly to the governess. 'I vow I sometimes think he can read minds!'

The children and Jacob preceded them from the room and, once they were out of earshot, Miss Patchett observed:

'I envisage a bright future for your young brother. He is an apt pupil and has a lively and enquiring mind!'

'I hope that you may be right,' said Caroline eagerly. 'David has always been somehow *different*! The rest of us are but mediocre scholars. I am afraid that I was as unacademic as Paula, as a child!'

Honoria Patchett turned mild brown eyes upon her and smiled.

'Even *I* do not claim that academic qualifications are absolutely necessary for a young lady!' she said. 'Do not demean your own abilities, my dear. You have many good qualities which have nothing at all to do with book-learning!' Caroline's eyes widened with amazement at this unexpected compliment, then she flushed deeply when Miss

Patchett added: 'Mr Mark is most impressed with you! He is so used to meeting heedless, flighty girls, whom fond mamas delight to hurl at his head!'

As they made their exit from the house, Caroline strove to regain her composure.

'Mr Grant is evidently a favourite of yours,' she said at length. 'Was he as good a scholar as David promises to be?'

There was no use in denying it, thought Caroline ruefully. Her sole reason for seeking the governess's company, had been the possibility that Marcus Grant might come under discussion. Now that the opportunity was here, she must not become tongue-tied and too embarrassed to take advantage of it! Honoria Patchett needed little persuasion to talk of her former pupil. Indeed, she seemed eager to do so.

'He was something of a tease to his sisters,' she revealed, 'and, indeed, to *me* also, when he was at High Crags for his school holidays.'

She talked on, with a reminiscent smile upon her face for Marcus' minor misemeanors. Caroline found she was listening avidly. When the governess at last fell silent, she said:

'Miss Patchett — Hubert Channing suggested that Mr Grant might have been attacked by a highwayman. He says that a neighbour of ours had his coach stopped and was robbed recently, but I cannot believe that Mr Grant's assailant was a highway robber. What do you think?'

The governess pursed her lips, thought, then shook her head definitely.

'Mr Mark was not robbed,' she said. 'I have discussed this unpleasant business with your tenants, Mr and Mrs Brown. Mr Brown was the first to discover Mr Mark lying injured and his opinion is that whoever did the shooting, took fright and fled without waiting to check if the victim still lived.'

'It was a shocking thing to have happened,' murmured Caroline, biting her lip. 'I do not think I will *ever* forget that dreadful evening we spent, waiting for news.'

As they neared the West Lodge, they could see that the children and the dog had come to a halt outside.

'Ah!' boomed Miss Patchett, in her disconcertingly loud voice. 'Here *is* Mr Mark! Now you may question him yourself, my dear! How happy to see him upon his feet again!'

Strictly speaking, Marcus Grant was not upon his feet at all. In fact he was sitting in the sunshine upon a bench outside the lodge door. He had been reading, but had set down his book readily enough when David and Paula ran up to greet him. By the time Miss Patchett and Caroline had joined them, Paula was seated upon Marcus' knee, David was sitting upon the bench and the pup, Soppy, was doing its utmost to overturn both the seat and its occupants. Hampered by the giggling Paula and the excited pup, Marcus attempted to rise at the ladies' approach.

'Children!' boomed the governess. 'Come — we must continue with our walk. Bring Blenkinsop, for he will be company for Jacob!'

Caroline was amazed to observe David and Paula obey with alacrity. It seemed that Miss Patchett's word was law. With never a grumble, the schoolroom party and the two dogs turned to go. Marcus Grant lifted an eyebrow comically when Caroline took an uncertain step away from the bench.

'Come — do not desert me!' he pleaded. 'Quimby has allowed me outside at last and I am feeling rather lonely and neglected!'

Honoria Patchett looked back and nodded cheerfully.

'Of course you must stay to cheer our invalid, Miss Caroline,' she said firmly. 'I have just been regaling her with your childhood mischiefs, Mr Mark! Perhaps you will fill in the parts that I omitted!'

Left alone with the convalescent, a hot flush rose in Caroline's cheeks. With a sudden grin of amusement, Marcus patted the seat beside him.

'Don't mind Patchy!' he advised. 'Come, sit down. It is quite proper,' he added solemnly, 'for Quimby is hovering just behind the open door to make sure you do not overtire me!'

His friendly, teasing manner made nonsense of standing on terms of stiff propriety. Caroline returned his smile shyly and seated herself upon the extreme end of the bench.

'I — I am glad to see you returned to health, sir,' she murmured. 'David has kept us informed of your progress. Is it known yet, who caused your injury? We have heard nothing of the culprit being brought to justice.'

Marcus frowned and shook his head.

'At first I was convinced that it was a deliberate attempt upon my life,' he admitted. 'Now, I am inclined to dismiss my assailant as a mere poacher potting at a rabbit. When he saw me fall, he must have feared me dead and made off before blame could be set on his shoulders.'

'Miss Patchett says that Mr Brown believes that is what happened,' nodded Caroline. She hesitated, then clenched her hands in her lap and added:

'Simon suggested that Arkwright and Bassett both have reason to bear you a grudge. You must admit the possibility.' Raising her blue eyes to his, she said earnestly: 'I do hope you may be right, Marc — Mr Grant! I would prefer to think you had merely been mistaken for a rabbit!'

'I wish you would call me Marcus,' he said solemnly. 'I am so unused to all this ceremony! I, too, wish I could put faith in the poacher theory but — '

He spread his hands and looked at her gravely.

'It would be a shocking thing, M — Marcus,' said Caroline unsteadily, 'if the attack was made as a direct result of all the good you have done for my family. Perhaps it would be better if you left us and returned to your own home.'

Marcus reached out for her hand and held it in both of his.

'Do you wish me to leave, Caroline?' he asked her softly. 'Come, do not be afraid to say what you feel.'

Her colour deepened and her hand quivered in his.

'Oh, *no* I — ' she began, then looked up, startled.

A horse was cantering down the drive. When the rider saw them, he reined in, lifted his lip in a sneer and said:

'I am happy to see you have recovered so quickly from your headache, Caroline! It would seem that company other than mine was all you sought!'

With that he struck his horse sharply and rode off through the open gate.

'And who,' said Marcus Grant, rising to his feet with a frown, 'was *that*?'

'Oh dear!' said Caroline helplessly. 'I had forgotten Hubert! He is our neighbour, Hubert Channing. He paid a call upon Mama and I — I excused myself, pleading a headache. He will be exceedingly cross with me!'

Marcus was still staring in the

direction taken by Channing's horse. When Caroline murmured that perhaps it was time she returned to the house, he did not attempt to detain her. He bade her a half-absent farewell and she was uncharacteristically piqued to see that he had lost all interest in their conversation. It was not until she was back in the house that she realised she had made no mention to Marcus of the possibility of there being a highwayman in the district.

8

Three days after Hubert Channing's visit, a letter arrived for Mrs Fortune. It was brought by a liveried servant who did not wait for an answer. Reading this missive threw Sophia into a state of near-panic.

'Oh, my dears!' she said to her daughters in failing tones. 'Oh — my nerves are quite shot to pieces! What *are* we to do?'

'Surely the King is not thinking of paying us a visit?' suggested Nicola impishly. 'Come, Mama, who sent the letter and why has it upset you in this way?'

'It is from your Great-Aunt Martha!' revealed Sophia. 'She scolds me for spurning her offer to house us all — indeed she words herself very *strongly* on the matter. She says she intends coming here to see for herself how we go on beneath Mr Grant's guardianship. Oh — it will not do, at all.'

'Oh dear!' murmured Caroline inadequately. 'But surely you can put her off, Mama? Write and tell her that Paula and David have the chickenpox! Surely that would serve to deter her? Tell her *anything* to prevent her from setting out to visit us!'

'It is too late for that,' moaned her mother. 'The servant did not even wait for a reply. I am convinced that Great-Aunt Martha must already be on her way here. Oh — what are we to do?'

'I am sure there is no need for you to be so anxious, Mama,' soothed Caroline. 'Great-Aunt Martha knew — and disapproved — of how we went on when Papa was alive. She must see nothing but improvement now that we have Mr Grant to see to our affairs. She cannot fail to be impressed! We must have a room prepared for her and entertain her pleasantly so that she sees all is well with us. Then she will return home and leave us in peace!'

'Yes,' nodded Nicola. 'She will see that Mr Grant manages things beautifully and that we are in good hands. She will not stay here long, Mama. You may depend upon it!'

'I do not share your confidence, my dears,' said Sophia uneasily. 'But I hope you may be right! Personally, I can place no dependence in her early departure! She will be acting out of character if she begins to approve of any of us!'

Knowing themselves powerless to prevent Great-Aunt Martha from coming, they were obliged to put plans in hand for her arrival. Miss Patchett was taken into the family's confidence and was warned that the children must be particularly quiet and pretty-behaved during the visit of their elderly relative, for she disliked noise of any kind and would be quick to show disapproval.

Simon, too, received his instructions from his anxious mother. She had not forgotten — nor forgiven — his attitude towards Marcus Grant and was not eager for him to display his deplorable lack of good manners before his great-aunt.

'The old lady hates me already!' said Simon cheerfully. 'I am sure I could do nothing to give her a worse opinion of me, so do not worry on that account, Mama!'

'You must not do anything stupid while she is here,' entreated Nicola. 'You see, if she thinks that Mr Grant cannot keep us all in order, she may well decide to interfere and I know that Mama will not stand up to her bullying! I, for one, do not wish to be parcelled off to live beneath *her* roof. Why — she would never consent to my wearing breeches!'

'I will be good!' promised her brother lightly. 'Although I have no opinion of Grant's guardianship, at least he does not get in my way as the old lady would do! I have no great desire to move out of the district. Things have livened up somewhat during these past few weeks.'

He went off, whistling gaily. Caroline frowned after her brother, wondering at his change of attitude. Apart from spending a deal of time with Cedric Channing, his way of life did not appear to have altered in the manner he suggested. Why then, should he seem more than satisfied with his lot, so soon after his fiery protests against Marcus Grant? By promising not to upset Great-Aunt Martha, he could almost be accused of accepting life beneath Grant's guardianship. It seemed somewhat out of character, pondered Caroline troubled, but at least he did not intend to upset the plan to soothe their great-aunt's doubts and fears.

It occurred to Caroline then, that Marcus Grant would be interested to hear of the impending arrival of their elderly relative. Indeed, she argued with herself, it was only proper that he should be warned that his guardianship was about to be contested by Great-Aunt Martha!

Always honest, Caroline felt obliged to admit satisfaction in having a valid excuse of seeking out Marcus Grant.

She was convinced that he had taken pleasure in his talk with her three days ago, but had seen nothing of him since then. The sight of Hubert Channing had caused him almost to forget her presence. She frowned to herself. Marcus was totally unlike anyone she had ever met before. He appeared to have little use for social civilities and seemed to prefer work to pleasure — surely an oddity in a *gentleman*? Perhaps work was his pleasure, she thought ruefully. He certainly seemed to enjoy the chance of ordering their lives to his own pattern! She had to admit trying to behave in a manner pleasing to him, knowing that his first impression of her had been that she was merely frivolous. Yet, she had had so little chance to show him that hers *was* a worthwhile nature! Was it really so important that he should think well of her, or was she merely piqued to find him seemingly impervious to her attraction? All she knew for certain was that Great-Aunt Martha's arrival must do nothing to cause the termination of Marcus' guardianship of the Fortune family. With this in mind, she set off down the drive, making for the West Lodge.

As she walked, Caroline noted the improvement caused by their careful cutting-back of the bushes and by the children's weeding of the gravelled drive. The task had been well worth the effort, she decided. Apart from keeping the roses in order and snipping off the dead flowers, there was little else to be done. Any heavier gardening was not really work for ladies and children, she thought, and poor Whitton could not be expected to cope with the grounds as well as the stables. No doubt Great-Aunt Martha would grumble on at length about the unkempt look of the place!

'But at least we have tried to do our part in improving our home, even if it *is* in a very small way,' murmured Caroline out loud. 'This is more than we ever did, before Marcus Grant came upon the scene!'

In most families, she mused, strict mourning would be observed, but Papa had always spoken against the taking-on of heavy blacks. She was sure he would not have objected to the way in which they were living, nor to the way in which they, his children were wearing colours again so soon after his demise. Apart from all other considerations, she argued mentally, a new dark-hued wardrobe for each member of the family was quite beyond their means!

As she approached the West Lodge, she became suddenly aware that a carriage was in the road outside the gates. Oh dear — had Great-Aunt Martha arrived already? Yet, wait — the gates stood open. Surely *her* coachman would have driven straight up the drive to the house? Caroline was puzzled and she quickened her step, coming to a halt beside the open gates.

The carriage was a fashionable lightweight vehicle drawn by a handsome pair of matched greys, which were fidgetting high-spiritedly beneath the hands of a servant. This was definitely not the heavy, cumbersome coach belonging to Great-Aunt Martha!

Even as Caroline watched from her position beside the gates, the lodge door opened and Marcus Grant came out. Of course, she thought then — the visitors had come to see Marcus, not the Fortune family. Marcus was not alone. There was a lady upon his arm. She was modishly dressed in a green travelling gown and was laughing up at him. Caroline shrank back against the further gatepost, willing that neither Marcus nor the lady should look across and find her staring at them. Suddenly, the door of the carriage opened and out stepped another lady. She was younger than the one with Marcus Grant and had curling dark hair and an exquisite pale-blue gown. With a cry of delight, which was quite audible to Caroline, the younger lady ran towards Marcus and threw her arms about him. With a sick feeling in the pit of her stomach, Caroline backed away, intending to slip between the bushes and make good her escape. Yet, even as she moved, Marcus looked up and their eyes met over the dark curls of his caller.

Caroline gave a sudden gasp, turned, lifted up her skirts and fled the length of the drive, not stopping until she had reached the roses upon the terrace. Scarcely knowing what she was doing, she began to gather a bunch of rosebuds. She was blinded by a sudden rush of tears and was pricking her fingers unmercifully. It was not until a particularly vicious thorn pierced her thumb, that she dropped the rosebuds and sped indoors to the sanctuary of her own room. Fortunately she saw no one and therefore comment was not passed upon her upset state.

The sight of that dark-haired beauty throwing herself so confidently upon Marcus Grant had pricked Caroline's self-assured bubble of content, as surely as the thorns had pricked her skin. Would the young lady have greeted

Marcus so familiarly unless she were his intended bride?

Then, suddenly, her brow cleared and she gave a shaky laugh. According to Miss Patchett, Marcus Grant had two sisters. What could be more natural than that they should visit their brother in his temporary home? Were his visitors merely *sisters*? She wondered hopefully if this might prove to be so.

Her reaction to the sight of that young lady in Marcus' arms had been one of fierce rejection and she pondered unsteadily on the unexpected depth of her own feeling for Marcus, which lay thus revealed. The realisation was a sobering one. She knew that he liked her a little, but she also knew that she must not begin to read too much into their few meetings, for that might lead to heartbreak.

Marcus knew that she had seen his visitors. If they were indeed his sisters, would he bring them up to the house? Would they wish to meet the family in his care?

Yet the day dragged on and no one came to call. Young David, a constant visitor at the lodge, was the only person to mention the ladies seen earlier by Caroline. According to the boy, Marcus Grant had been visited by his sister, Mrs Ratcliffe and a 'pretty lady' who was her friend. Caroline's spirits sank even lower than before. She knew she must accept that the elder lady in green was Marcus' sister. Who, then, was the dark-haired lady in blue who knew him well enough to greet him in that excessively familiar manner?

* * *

Great-Aunt Martha arrived at Fortune Hall on the evening of the following day. She did not pause to disapprove of the condition of either house or grounds. She did not even pause to make disparaging remarks about each and every member of the family, in her normal disconcerting manner.

Instead, she greeted her unwilling

hostess with a demand that she should be shown to her appointed room without delay and a further demand that a tray be sent in, which contained something rather stronger than *tea*!

'For,' said Great-Aunt Martha irefully, with a martial light in her pale-blue eyes, 'I have been set-upon by *highwaymen*! I have suffered a shock to my entire system and must rest before I decide upon the steps to be taken!'

The old lady seemed furiously angry, rather than shocked, confided Nicola mischievously to Caroline. Just imagine — a highwayman having the temerity to call a halt to Great-Aunt Martha's coach! She had probably given him the length of her tongue instead of the purse he desired!

Caroline found she could not even summon up a smile for her sister's wit. Her mind was still fully concentrated on the problem of her own emotions and Marcus Grant's visitor of yesterday.

9

Great-Aunt Martha did not approve of conversation at the breakfast table, so nothing was learned of her ordeal of the previous evening until the meal was over.

Sophia Fortune ushered her elderly relative into the drawing-room and Caroline followed. Nicola was now obliged to ascend to the schoolroom and begged her sister to hearken to all the details, so that she in turn might be regaled with them. To Caroline's surprise, Simon followed into the drawing-room and went over to sit on the window-seat. It seemed out of character that he should seek the old lady's company, but he was probably curious about her encounter with highwaymen.

'Who is the nearest Justice of the Peace?' demanded Miss Martha Fortune without further preamble. 'I have been discussing this shocking matter with Thwaite and we feel an urgency in reporting the occurrence to someone in authority. No self-styled 'gentleman of the road' is going to halt *my* coach then escape with impunity! I told the rascal my opinion of him to his face and you may be sure that I did not mince my words!'

Thwaite was Great-Aunt Martha's undersized personal maid, who travelled everywhere with her. Caroline guessed from past experience that the elderly maid would not have had much opportunity to voice her own opinion, in the discussion with her mistress. It would be Martha Fortune herself who felt an urgent need to report last night's incident!

'Oh dear, this is a shocking thing to have happened to you,' murmured Sophia helplessly.

'Indeed yes!' retorted Miss Fortune brusquely. 'Come now, Sophia — the name of your local Justice of the Peace, if you please! I intend to report the matter and to demand a satisfactory investigation from him.'

A muffled sound came from the direction of the window-seat. Fortunately Great-Aunt Martha did not appear to notice, but Caroline frowned across and was astonished to see that Simon had been overcome by some form of emotion. He had turned his head away, but she had a strong suspicion that her brother was actually *laughing*.

'Oh dear!' repeated Sophia inadequately. 'I believe Sir Luke Channing must be the man you seek, for he is both a Justice of the Peace and our near neighbour.'

Simon *was* laughing, thought Caroline uneasily. What was amusing about having the highwayman's exploits reported to Sir Luke?

'Sir Luke Channing?' said Miss Fortune and nodded her grey head. She sat up straight-backed in her black silk gown and fixed Sophia with a steely glance. 'Now — tell me all you have heard of the activities of highwaymen in this district. Then we may decide what is known of the man — or rather *men*, for he was not alone — who stopped my coach last night. I must be sure of my facts before I make my report.'

Caroline, who was still looking across at her brother, saw Simon grow watchful and knew that he was no longer amused.

'Ah — oh dear!' began Sophia yet again. Poor Mama was never at her best with their great-aunt, thought Caroline sympathetically, forgetting Simon for the moment. Sophia made a visible effort to pull herself together and went on: 'I believe Mr Marriott was robbed by a highwayman recently. We heard this from Hubert Channing, Sir Luke's own son. Then, of course, there was the unpleasant attack upon poor Marcus Grant. We still do not know who was responsible for that.'

'Is that all?' queried Martha Fortune incredulously. 'I was convinced you would tell me no one was safe abroad at nights in these parts. Does the holding-up of my coach form merely the *third* of these outrages?'

'Actually, you may be only the second victim, Great-Aunt Martha,' said Caroline apologetically. 'As far as we can be sure, Marcus Grant was not attacked by a highwayman, at all!'

Martha Fortune gave Caroline an intimidating frown as if questioning her right to speak.

'I was addressing your mother,' she pointed out severely, then added slowly: 'Marcus Grant? Ah, yes! He is the man to take on this ridiculous guardianship-affair, is he not? I am convinced you did not enquire into the young man's background, Sophia, before you made him free of your home!'

'I — oh — Henry named Marcus in his will,' defended poor Sophia weakly. 'Marcus is a — a distant connection of ours and I am sure that his background must be unimpeachable.'

Great-Aunt Martha gave vent to a sound suspiciously like a snort.

'Unimpeachable? Fiddlesticks!' she scoffed. 'I see you have not heard about the scandalous nature of his elopement two years ago? Ah, yes — ' she went on in satisfied tones when she saw their astonished faces. 'I see I must enlighten you! Your trustworthy Mr Grant is nothing but a petty fortune-hunter! He ran off with the heiress Alicia Dawes — Mr Wingate Dawes' only child — and only her father's timely intervention prevented the *worst* from happening!'

Simon rose from his seat and sauntered over to join the group.

'So the saintly Grant has faults after all, has he?' he enquired with malicious glee.

Martha Fortune gave him a glacial look.

'Who gave you leave to speak, sir?' she snapped. 'I see your manners have not suffered improvement since last we met! Really, Sophia — do you not *despair* of your children? I own I can see little to admire in your upbringing of them. And where are Nicola, David and

Paula? Why do they not come to greet their poor old aunt who has travelled so far to see them? I imagine they are wasting their time as usual with that pudding of a nursemaid?'

Sophia Fortune was very pale, but she held her chin high and said quietly:

'The children are up in the schoolroom with their governess, Miss Patchett. I am sure they are applying themselves most diligently to their lessons. Miss Patchett has great hopes of D — David's intelligence and Paula can already read a little!'

Bravo, Mama, applauded Caroline silently, wishing she dared to say the words aloud. How *could* Great-Aunt Martha be so overbearing and rude?

'Governess?' snapped Miss Fortune. 'What nonsense is this, Sophia? How can you afford to pay a governess, when foolish Henry left you burdened with nothing but debt?'

Sophia opened her mouth wearily to reply. Suddenly tears stung her eyes and her spark of courage was extinguished.

She said nothing.

'Mr Grant tells us that we are now free of debt,' said Caroline quietly. 'As to Miss Patchett — perhaps you would care to go up to the schoolroom to see how the children go on? I will take you up there now, if it is your wish. I am sure Miss Patchett will spare us a moment from the routine of her lessons!'

Martha Fortune glared at her great-niece.

'Do not be pert with me, miss!' she advised harshly. 'You have a pretty enough face, girl, but you will never catch a husband until you learn to quell that unladylike forwardness of manner!'

Caroline kept a firm rein upon tongue and temper.

'As we are still in mourning for Papa, I do not feel that the question of my marrying is important,' she said quietly.

'Mourning? Hah!' retorted Miss Fortune. 'From the sight of you in that *blue* gown, miss, I had thought *mourning* was far from your mind!'

Caroline went very pale and stared at the old lady until she had the grace to look away.

'I have but one black gown,' said Caroline. 'Papa disliked black and even had he not done so, there is no money to purchase new clothing for any of us at this moment.'

'Ah — quite so!' muttered Martha Fortune.

Caroline took a deep steadying breath.

'I believe we were discussing the highwayman,' she pointed out, determinedly polite.

'Yes,' put in Simon quickly. 'Do describe the fellow, ma'am! Would you know him if you saw him again, do you think?'

They had succeeded in changing the subject, for Great-Aunt Martha said frostily:

'There is nothing wrong with either my eyesight or my memory, young sir! The villain was tall and broad-shouldered. Naturally he wore a mask which concealed his face and his hat was worn low. I cannot describe his features but certainly I would know him again! However, his companion — or *companions* — stood in shadow.'

'Tall and broad-shouldered,' repeated Simon. Caroline caught a hint of relief in his tone but forgot this when he added solemnly: 'I think perhaps you are describing our family guardian, Great-Aunt Martha! Perhaps he is a highwayman, as well as being a fortune-hunter, ma'am?'

Miss Fortune did not deign to reply to this levity.

'I will now retire to my room, Sophia,' she said. 'Naturally I must *trust* that the children are hard at work. I am by far too old to go traipsing up all those stairs to the schoolroom. Thwaite and I will write down all we can recall of last night, for even *details* can prove to be important. After luncheon, we will seek out Sir Luke Channing and order him to apprehend the villains who are preying upon honest travellers! Of course, they took nothing from *me* as I held on to my purse and gave them my round opinion of their behaviour! However, others may be less strong-minded than I, so I must apprise Sir Luke of the position!'

'Well, you can't do that today, ma'am!' said Simon quickly. 'Sir Luke is from home. His son, Cedric, is my friend, you see, and I know for fact that his father is away at the moment!'

'Then I shall wait!' announced Martha Fortune regally. 'Simon — your arm, if you please! You may escort me up to my room!'

With a comical look across his shoulder for his sister, Simon obeyed. Left alone with her daughter, Sophia Fortune rose to her feet and clenched her hands tightly.

'What are we to do, Caroline?' she implored tremulously. 'I cannot even *talk* to her without shaking in my shoes! My thoughts fly out of my head when I attempt to answer her. She has never had any opinion of me from the day I married your poor, dear Papa! Oh — and what of this shocking thing she has told us of Marcus? What are we to say to *that*?'

Caroline tried to summon up a smile.

'Mr Grant's personal past has no bearing on the way in which he is managing our affairs, Mama,' she said quietly. 'After all — his *private* life does not really affect us!'

Her mother sat down again and gave her a doubtful look.

'Ah — but I have been so *hopeful* of you and Marcus,' she said mournfully. 'He seems so *right* for you, love! I know you do not dislike him as you at first professed. Come, admit it, love! You like Marcus, do you not? But it will not *do* at all, if he has behaved scandalously.'

'If he is really a fortune-hunter,' said Caroline with an attempt at a shrug, 'then he will not look twice at me for, who knows better than he, how our finances lie? Fortune is merely my *name*! Even if Great-Aunt Martha has confused him with someone else and he is quite blameless, then he still may never come to regard me in the light which you desire, Mama! *My* opinion of *him* has nothing to say in the matter! Now come, I feel you must lie down in your room for a time. Your nerves are shattered, love!'

'Yes, I suppose I must rest,' agreed her mother wearily, 'if only to prepare myself for Great-Aunt Martha's next onslaught against my sensibilities!'

When she was alone, Caroline went out on to the terrace and gazed unseeingly at the roses.

It seemed that the incident she had observed yesterday at the West Lodge and Great-Aunt Martha's revelation must add together to cast new light upon the character of Marcus Grant, she thought unhappily. Perhaps it would have been best for all concerned if he had refused the guardianship, as had been his original intention. Instead of which —

'Caroline,' said a voice quietly and she turned with a flurry of blue skirts to find herself facing the subject of her thoughts.

'Oh, M — Marcus!' she stammered, then rushed on: 'I am glad to see you! Our great-aunt arrived last night and I fear she intends to question your guardianship of us. She — she offered earlier to house us all, you see, and Mama refused, saying we would stay on here as Papa wished and have you to c — care for us — ' She broke off and turned her head from him, distress robbing her of the power of speech.

Gently Marcus put his hands upon her shoulders and made her face him again.

'You are upset, love,' he said accusingly. 'Is this great-aunt of yours something of a dragon? I must waste no time in meeting her. Perhaps when she sees me she will realise that I am capable of guiding your affairs.'

Caroline lifted troubled blue eyes to his.

'Marcus — she does not *like* you,' she said unsteadily.

He smiled and bent his head to drop a light kiss on her forehead.

'Don't be foolish, love,' he advised lightly. 'She has never met me so how can she hold me in dislike?'

'She t — told us about Alicia Dawes,' said Caroline in a choked whisper.

Marcus released her abruptly and he gave a frown.

'Your elderly aunt is remarkably well-informed,' he murmured. 'Why, it was but yesterday that my sister brought Alicia to call upon me! I think you saw her, love, and I was about to explain the matter.'

'Yesterday?' gasped Caroline. 'Then *that* was her?'

Marcus gave her a long look and frowned again.

'I think we are at cross-purposes,' he suggested.

Caroline gave a small cry of distress.

'Great-Aunt Martha told us of y — your elopement with Miss Dawes two years ago,' she managed. '*That* was bad enough but now you tell me that she came to see you as recently as yesterday. Oh, Marcus, please — I must go!'

She turned to flee indoors but he was too quick for her.

'No, love!' he said, holding her firmly by the shoulders. 'We will not have these tiresome misunderstandings, you and I!'

He kissed her again, half-angrily, this time full upon her lips, but she pushed him away fiercely, remembering how only yesterday she had seen him embraced by Alicia Dawes.

'*I* am not an heiress, Marcus Grant!' she said stormily. 'Let me go this *instant*!'

He released her as rapidly as if she had slapped his face and stared after her as she ran into the house. Then, with a heavy sigh, he went back to the West Lodge.

'And what is wrong with us on this bright summer morning?' greeted his manservant bracingly, at the door.

Marcus scowled.

'Quimby,' he said gloomily. 'I am

almost decided upon becoming a *woman-hater*!'

'Oh — is that all?' said his manservant with undisguised relief. 'I thought something was *really* amiss, Mr Mark!'

10

Martha Fortune seemed unusually subdued at the luncheon hour and toyed with her bread and butter and fruit in an uncharacteristic manner. Therefore it came not as a complete surprise when Thwaite announced a little later that her elderly mistress was indisposed.

'Oh, no!' said Sophia in distress, then added rather more brightly: 'Perhaps she will be confined to her room for several days!'

'Mama!' rebuked Caroline with a chuckle. 'That is very naughty of you. Well, I suppose one of us must go up to see her?'

Nicola rose hastily to her feet.

'I am just going out to help Whitton with the horses,' she said and made good her escape.

'With your permission, Mama, I will

ride over to Channing House now,' said Simon, edging towards the door. 'You recall that I am to stay there for the night with Cedric and Hubert?'

'Yes — no! I recall nothing of the sort!' protested his mother. 'Well — I suppose you must go if they are expecting you, but it is very bad of you to leave just when Great-Aunt Martha is ill.'

Simon gave Caroline a wink.

'My presence would scarcely aid the old lady's recovery,' he said solemnly. 'I am convinced I am bad for her nerves, even when she is well!'

With that he left the room.

'Caro — would you — ?' began her mother hopefully.

Her daughter gave a rueful smile.

'Yes, Mama!' she said dutifully. 'One of us must go up to see how she does. I will go to her *and* I will hold my tongue if she is rude to me!'

However, Martha Fortune was in no state for caustic comment. When Caroline tapped and entered, she found her great-aunt lying back upon a mound [illegible]

'Oh, Miss Caroline,' said the little woman in distress. 'Madam seems so much worse now. I fear she has had some form of *attack*. What are we to do?'

Martha Fortune pressed a large-knuckled hand to her ribs and moaned.

'Get me a doctor, girl,' she said in a cracked whisper. 'I fear I am dying!'

The village doctor, who had attended Nicola on the day of Marcus Grant's arrival, was hastily summoned. Although brusque in manner and no waster of words, he seemed efficient enough.

'Heart,' he told Thwaite and Caroline. 'A mild enough attack this time. There may be others. Keep her off her feet and on a light diet and don't thwart her or quarrel with her. With care she'll be herself again in a few weeks time.'

‘A few *weeks*?’ said Sophia Fortune, aghast, when the news was reported to her. ‘I suppose she cannot be taken home to be ill *there*?’

‘No, of course she must not be moved,’ said Caroline. ‘Now, you are not to concern yourself, Mama. Thwaite and I will manage and we can always call in Dr Stephenson again, if Great-Aunt Martha takes a turn for the worse. He has told us what to do. Now — do not worry! You know that you are no good in a sickroom, Mama!’

‘I suppose we should tell Marcus,’ said her mother next.

‘Why?’ asked Caroline sharply. ‘Great-Aunt Martha’s illness has nothing whatsoever to do with him. Now, do not be inviting him up to the house, Mama, for I do not wish to see him!’

‘What ails you, love?’ said her mother in perplexity. ‘I thought — ’

‘Do not have any thoughts connecting me with that — with Marcus Grant,’ said Caroline flatly. ‘I have no opinion of him and I never wish to speak with him again! That is the *end* of it. Mama.' [illegible] lessons so that there was little chance of disturbing the invalid. Simon took advantage of the situation, by sending a servant over from Channing House to collect some of his clothing, so that he might prolong his stay with his friend, Cedric.

'I suppose he is best out of the way, until Great-Aunt Martha is a little better,' agreed his mother, only half attending to the matter.

Caroline was kept too busy in her role of sickroom attendant to worry about the doings of her brother. Martha Fortune made a petulant invalid, demanding to be read to and fetched and carried for, until Caroline was exhausted and fit only to drop into her bed each night. Yet, it did not occur to her to grumble, for Thwaite's lot was heavier by far than her own.

Someone, probably young David, had apprised Marcus Grant of the situation, for he arrived at the house with a plentiful supply of eggs and butter from the estate farms, for the invalid. He learned from Sophia that Caroline had no wish to see him, but chose to make no comment upon the fact, to Sophia's intense curiosity. Indeed, he seemed more interested to learn that Simon was staying at Channing House.

'I fear Miss Fortune's highwayman has halted another coach,' said Marcus next. 'It seems that this time, he has made a considerable haul of gold and jewellery from a family who were travelling south to London.'

'How very shocking,' murmured Sophia, giving the matter only cursory attention. 'Great-Aunt Martha shows a little improvement at last, according to Caroline. Soon,' she said gloomily, 'we will have her down in the drawing-room with us.'

Sophia Fortune was an incredibly

selfish person, decided Marcus impa- [illegible]

'Why, no!' she said with a shake of her head. 'Whatever gave you that idea, Marcus? Great-Aunt Martha dislikes us all impartially! Caro is merely doing her duty in helping in the sickroom. My own nerves would not stand for it, you see, and Nico is a thought young, even if she were *not* fully occupied with the schoolroom and the horses.'

'Simon is being little help to you by absenting himself from home, is he?' observed Marcus with a frown.

'Great-Aunt Martha has no time at all for Simon,' said Sophia cheerfully. 'He grates upon her nerves at every turn!'

'So the load must fall upon Caroline?' murmured Marcus, with a lift of a dark brow.

'Yes, of course it must,' said her mother comfortably. 'She is the eldest of my children, after all!'

Marcus gave her a long, thoughtful look, then turned the subject.

'I have given Bassett work at Hazel Farm,' he said. 'He is a lazy, idle-minded fellow, but he has a family to support and, after all, I did cause his removal from his position of gate-keeper. It is really up to me to see him employed, is it not?'

'Oh — of course you must do as you think fit, my dear,' said Sophia. 'I have the utmost confidence in your judgment and I am sure *I* do not understand estate matters at all.'

Marcus gave a wry grin.

'My judgment warns me not to give employment to Will Arkwright,' he said. 'I had hoped giving him notice to quit the farm would remove him from the neighbourhood, but it seems I was over-optimistic! He is living in the village and has taken a room in the blacksmith's home. He glares blackly

whenever he sees me and I have th[illegible]
feeling that h[illegible]

[illegible] wish to [illegible] conversation and had no desire to talk on affairs of the estate, for she was fidgetting a little with a fold of her gown and not giving him her full attention. Politely but ruefully, Marcus took his leave of her.

He made his way to the South Lodge. The Browns were good tenants as he had known they would be. They were not in constant residence at the lodge and he knew they had just arrived back once more from a sojourn in town to attend to Mr Brown's business affairs. Sophia Fortune had probably forgotten the very existence of the tenants, mused Marcus, although the rent of the lodge was being a considerably useful aid to the finances of the Fortune family!

The Browns had transformed the

small, child-trampled garden to the rear of the South Lodge and, already, it made a pleasing sight to the eyes. Mrs Brown had brought a favourite yellow rose-bush from her town garden and was carefully persuading it to enjoy the change to richer soil. Quimby had brought flowering plants over from High Crags for both of the lodge gardens and so the west and the south entrances had each taken on an improved and brighter appearance.

'Good day to you, Mr Grant, sir,' Marcus was greeted by Mabel Brown. 'Will you take tea or coffee with us?'

'Happen he'd prefer a glass o' wine with me, Mabel-love!' smiled her husband.

Marcus set the problems of the Fortune family behind him and went into the lodge to take refreshment with the Browns.

Conversation soon turned to the activities of the highwayman. It seemed that the holding-up of the coach had happened on the very road where they had travelled on their recent return to [illegible]

had wi' them,' said Mabel Brown sympathetically. 'Ah, well — yon highwayman-fellow will be caught afore long an' he'll be hanged an' then we'll all rest easy again!'

Marcus gave a thoughtful nod and sipped at his wine. Somehow he was thinking more of Caroline Fortune than of the highwayman. He gave a sigh, knowing how easily misunderstandings came about and how difficult they were to resolve. It was evident that Caroline had chosen to think the very worst of him. He remembered the hurt look in her eyes and winced visibly.

'Wine a mite sharp to your taste, Mr Grant?' asked Albert Brown noticing his caller's expression.

'The wine is very good,' said Marcus

reassuringly. 'I was about to enquire the name of your wine-merchant,' he added mendaciously.

'Is that shoulder still troubling you, sir?' said Mabel Brown solicitously. 'T'villain as did *that* to you should be hanged — indeed he should!'

This emphasis on the death-penalty accorded ill with a persistent thought at the back of Marcus' mind and he winced anew. Feeling slightly sick, he made his farewells, blaming his healed wound for his mood of distraction.

11

[illegible] galloped across the moor, the wind whistling in her ears and her long fair hair streaming out unconfined behind her. It was good to have an opportunity of riding alone, without Whitton at her side entreating her to take care, she thought rejoicingly. It was a pity that her ride would take her no further than Channing House, but at least she was able to come the long way round and enjoy a little freedom! She gave a small grimace. It was horrid at home just now, with Great-Aunt Martha so ill and everyone saying 'hush' at every turn. Poor Caro was looking quite peaked and done-in, she thought, glad that *she* had not been detailed for sickroom duties.

This errand was more to her liking! Mama had asked her to ride over and find out how much longer Simon intended staying with the Channings. As Mama had neglected to mention that Whitton must accompany her, she was taking the advantage of giving Hermes his head.

Eventually, she turned with some regret towards Channing House. Mama would suspect she had been up to mischief if she dallied too long upon her errand!

The Channing home was as understaffed as her own and Nicola saw no sign of servants when she arrived in the cobbled stableyard. Used to coping alone, she secured Hermes beneath the shade of a tree outside the stableyard and went round towards the front of the house on foot, a slender boyish figure in her cherished breeches and an old shirt of Simon's. Mama had also forgotten to remind her to wear her hated riding-habit!

The Channing's rose-terrace was in a shocking state, she thought, pushing past jutting bushes and pausing in the

overgrown wilderness. It was a wond[illegible]
there were [illegible]

[illegible] had, as yet,
[illegible] no one, Nicola decided she might as well enter here into the library, instead of announcing herself formally at the main door. She did not stand in awe of the Channings and knew that Sir Luke, at least, had a fondness for her. Never having had a daughter, he was inclined to make much of her, praising her seat upon a horse and saying she was more of a man than either of his weakling sons! However, she had not seen Sir Luke for some time and knew he was still from home.

In the act of entering the house, she paused uncertainly as voices reached her from the library. It would not do to present herself before visitors, clad as she was in her breeches! She listened for a moment, then decided that the voices belonged to her own brother and Cedric Channing. She insinuated herself round the partly open door and stood concealed behind the floor-length curtains.

Simon and Cedric were in here, no doubt plotting mischief. It would do no harm to listen for a while, before she went in, thought Nicola with a complete lack of scruple. She risked a peep round the curtain and saw that her brother and Cedric were seated at a table quite close to the window. She held her breath and watched Cedric. He was unrolling what appeared to be a bulky, velvet-covered bundle, upon the table. Then the contents of the bundle lay revealed, Nicola's blue eyes flew wide with shock and she bit hard on the back of her hand to stifle a desire to exclaim aloud.

Ears strained in earnest now and face pale, she listened to what the two youths were saying. When she was entirely sure in her own mind of the import of what she had seen and heard, she made a stealthy exit, tiptoed back through the overgrown roses, then ran headlong to where she had left Hermes tethered. Thankfully [illegible] behind the tree. Hermes reared and almost unseated Nicola, but she clung on to his neck and gazed down in shock at the narrowed, suspicious eyes of Will Arkwright, the farmer dismissed by Marcus Grant.

'Nay — an' what's t'big hurry, young miss?' he said, reaching out a huge hand for Hermes' reins.

With a gasp of sheer panic, Nicola grabbed at the trailing reins and urged her mount into a gallop, careless of Arkwright's safety. The man narrowly missed being struck by Hermes' hooves and he scowled consideringly after the fleeing girl. Then, rubbing his unshaven cheek with a horny thumb, he frowned to himself and entered the stableyard of Channing House.

* * *

Nicola shook her head dumbly at Quimby when he offered her a glass of fruit-cup.

'No,' she said at last, when the manservant persisted, alarmed by her upset state. 'No — I do not need anything, Quimby — only to speak with Mr Grant. I *must* see him! Where is he? Do you think he will be long in returning?'

The manservant cocked an ear towards the door, then nodded.

'That sounds like him now, miss,' he said.

Nicola flew across the room and grasped Marcus by the sleeve as he entered.

'Mr Grant! Something *terrible* is happening,' she began. 'I have just been over to Channing House and — '

She broke off with a gasp and fell silent. Marcus Grant was not alone. Two ladies were standing behind him in the tiny hall of the lodge.

'Well, Marcus? Who is your little friend?' asked the elder lady in placid, comfortable tones.

Marcus gave Nicola a tiny warning shake of his head and she knew he was telling her that her news must wait.

'Nicola,' he said, 'this is my sister, Mrs Ratcliffe. She has driven over to visit me. Louisa — this is Nicola Fortune.'

'What about me, Marcus, dear?' asked a plaintive voice.

Nicola looked beyond Mrs Ratcliffe and saw the most beautiful young lady she had ever set eyes upon. Belatedly, she remembered her breeches and the fact that her hair was hanging in a tangled mass down her back. She flushed deeply. The younger visitor was a vision of loveliness from the carefully arranged curls of her dark hair, to the tips of the slippers which peeped from beneath her elegant rose-coloured gown.

'Oh! Oh — I am sorry to intrude,' breathed poor Nicola in a low shamed voice.

Marcus took her hand in a warm, reassuring clasp.

'Nico,' he said calmly, 'this is Alicia Dawes. She is a friend of my sister and is staying with her for a time.'

'I am a friend of *Louisa's* only? Oh, Marcus!' pouted Miss Dawes prettily.

'Nicola helps with the horses, Louisa, if you are querying her attire,' went on Marcus blithely. 'Louisa, too, was fond of breeches, when she was your age, Nico!'

Mrs Ratcliffe smiled and although her colouring was fairer than her brother's, Nicola saw that their eyes were similar and she found herself relaxing slightly.

'Louisa! You — in breeches?' gasped Miss Dawes, her eyes wide.

'That was a very long time ago and it is naughty of Marcus to speak of it, now that I am a respectable married lady!' smiled Mrs Ratcliffe.

Marcus put a hand upon Nicola's shoulder.

'Now, I can see that some kind of crisis has arisen, for Nico to come here in such haste,' he said. 'Quimby

[illegible]

small garden. 'You look quite charming in your breeches, you know! Alicia scarcely knows one end of a horse from the other — that is the reason why she would never dream of dressing as you do! Now — what is amiss? Is everyone well up at the house? Perhaps the old lady has taken a turn for the worse? Is the doctor needed? Shall I go for him?'

Nicola took a deep, steadying breath.

'No one is ill, Mr Grant,' she said. 'Oh — I have something *terrible* to tell you! Mama sent me over to Channing House, to ask Simon when he means to come home and — and,' she gulped and suddenly her blue eyes filled with tears. 'Oh — it is so very dreadful!' she wailed.

'It is Simon, is it not?' asked Marcus, suddenly alert.

Nicola mopped at her eyes with the back of her hand, then accepted the snowy linen handkerchief Marcus silently held out to her.

'I overheard Simon and Cedric Channing talking,' she went on bleakly. 'I listened carefully and I know there can be no mistake — no other explanation. Yes, I heard what they said — and I saw what was on the table between them.'

Patiently, Marcus drew the whole of the tale from the shaken girl. Every word she spoke, only served to confirm his own earlier suspicions.

'Did anyone see you arrive or leave Channing House?' he asked urgently, when she fell silent.

'No — yes!' said Nicola, biting on her lip. 'That horrid Will Arkwright was outside by the stables. He tried to stop me leaving, but I urged Hermes on and rode straight here to find you.'

'Arkwright?' said Marcus thoughtfully. 'Now I wonder if he has a part in all of this?'

'Probably!' agreed Nicola bitterly. 'Oh [illegible] into a pretty gown, wash the tears from your face and pretend all is well. I shall deal with Master Simon, never fear!'

She gave him a relieved and obedient nod.

'But what must I tell Mama?' she asked him trustfully. 'You see, she sent me with a message for Simon.'

'Tell her that you could not find your brother,' suggested Marcus. 'Now, remember what I have said, Nico. I must go back in to my guests now.'

Nicola nodded and tried to smile at him.

'She — she is very beautiful, isn't she?' she said in a subdued tone.

'Who is beautiful?' he said obtusely. 'Oh — do you mean Alicia? Well, I suppose you might say that, but it is really all a matter of taste, little one!'

'Then is she not to *your* taste?' asked Nicola innocently. 'I would say that *you* are to *hers*! I would think that any gentleman would be quite bowled over by her looks.'

'Perhaps, then, I am just not *any* gentleman,' said Marcus lightly. 'Go now, Nicola and do as I bade you. Keep a still tongue on all you saw and heard this afternoon.'

Obeying Marcus to the letter, Nicola went quickly to her own room, washed and put on a simple cotton gown. She was relieved to find that her mother did not delve too deeply into why she had been unable to give Simon the message. Sophia, it appeared, had more urgent worries than her elder son upon her mind.

'Great-Aunt Martha has announced her intention of joining us again tomorrow,' she said with a frown. 'She will not heed me, when I tell her she would be wise to rest longer. I can see that she is determined to inflict her presence — and her sharp tongue [illegible]

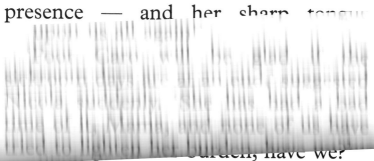

[illegible] burden, have we?'

Sophia stared at her in astonishment.

'It is not as if any of us actually *like* Great-Aunt Martha, my love,' she pointed out. 'It is not our fault that she chose to fall ill in our home. No one invited her to come, after all! We will all be glad when she is well enough to leave us.'

Nicola sighed, feeling unequal to the task of dealing with Mama's kind of logic.

'Yes, I suppose we will be glad to see her go,' admitted the girl honestly. 'Mama — has she spoken again of telling Sir Luke about the — the highwaymen?'

Sophia shook her head, then gave her daughter a searching look.

'You are quite pale, Nico love,' she

accused. 'The ride to Channing House should have put colour into your cheeks. Instead, you are white as a sheet. I *do* hope that you are not beginning to sicken for something, my dear? One invalid in the house is quite enough!'

Sometimes, thought Nicola, sometimes her mother could sound completely heartless! She bit on her lip, wondering how Mama would react when she was told of Simon's folly. If only Marcus could deal with the matter quietly. Perhaps, then, Mama would never need to know the dreadful truth!

12

[illegible] at the breakfast table next morning. 'I am not needed now, it seems! Thwaite is to get Great-Aunt Martha down to the drawing-room later and will no longer require my services in the sickroom!'

'You look washed-out, Caro,' observed her sister with more truth than tact. 'It's a fine, sunny morning. Why not go out for a ride? I am sure you could do with the fresh air, after being cooped up indoors for so long!'

The two girls were alone at the table. Miss Patchett had already eaten her meal and gone up to the schoolroom, with a reminder to Nicola not to dally too long. Mrs Fortune had decided to lie late in her bed, to prepare herself for the ordeal of the descent of her elderly relative.

Caroline gave Nicola a keen glance.

'You seem a trifle on edge, Nico,' she observed. 'I hope you are not going to be ill. I am sure that I cannot be paler than *you* at this moment. Come, tell me, love! Is something troubling you?'

Nicola gave a heavy sigh.

'Yes,' she admitted wretchedly. 'Something is *very* wrong, Caro! Oh — I must not tell you. I promised Marcus Grant that I would hold my tongue!'

Caroline stiffened.

'Marcus Grant?' she said. 'What is all the mystery, love? Surely you may tell me if even *Marcus Grant* is aware of it?'

Nicola left the table and went to ensure that the dining-room door was properly closed. Then she returned to her sister's side.

'It is Simon!' she whispered. 'He is in the most *shocking* scrape, Caro! I dare not think where this might all end.'

Caroline grew impatient.

'I think you must tell me about it, Nico,' she coaxed. 'If Simon is up to no good, then it concerns the *family* far more than it concerns Mr Grant.'

[illegible] have truly been carrying out highway robbery, you see. Mama sent me over to Channing House with a message. I overheard them talking and I saw a heap of jewels and coins that they had stolen. I went to tell Marcus Grant. I thought he should know.'

Caroline stared in shock.

'You are quite sure of this, Nico?' she asked at last.

'Yes — oh *yes!*' said Nicola miserably. 'There can be no mistake. M — Marcus said he would deal with the matter and I was to say nothing. Oh, I have broken my promise! I *said* I would keep quiet about what I knew!'

Caroline dismissed Marcus Grant with an airy wave of her hand.

'Tell me all you saw and heard, Nico,' she said urgently. 'Simon must be crazed! What can he be thinking of? There is only one penalty for highway robbery. Does he want to end up on the *scaffold*?'

Haltingly, Nicola told her tale. When she reached the part where she had arrived at the West Lodge, she said slowly:

'Marcus Grant had two ladies calling upon him, Caro. They were very fine and I felt quite a hoyden in my breeches. One of them was his sister, Mrs Ratcliffe, but the other was a beautiful young lady called — '

'Alice Dawes?' supplied Caroline, her lips tightening.

Nicola gave her a startled look.

'Yes, that was her name,' she agreed. 'Have you met her then, Caro? How can you know her name?'

'I have not exactly *met* her,' said her sister levelly, 'but I have seen her. As you say, she is quite beautiful.'

'Well, Marcus does not like her above half!' disclosed Nicola eagerly. 'He as good as told me so!'

'Did he also tell you that he eloped with that [illegible]

[illegible] said Nicola indignantly. 'Well, anyway, this Alicia person called yesterday. How can you have *seen* her, Caro? You have been tied to the sickroom for days now.'

'Miss Dawes has been to the West Lodge before,' said Caroline wearily. 'In fact, it is possible that she is a frequent visitor there. Why should we know — or care, about her? It is of no interest whatsoever to me, love!'

Nicola gave her a sceptical look but forebore to comment.

'Oh — I will have to *fly* up to the schoolroom!' she said suddenly. 'Miss Patchett is very strict about punctuality. Please promise me you will not tell Marcus that I broke my word to him?' she begged from the doorway.

Caroline nodded.

'I promise that I will say nothing at all to *Mr Grant*,' she said firmly. 'Do not fret on that score, love!'

Left alone, Caroline mused on her sister's revelations until her head ached. Regrettably, she found her thoughts leaving the terrible problem of Simon and turning to the less important matter of Miss Alicia Dawes.

'Nico was right,' she said aloud at last. 'I must go out of doors for a while. I have had no fresh air for days!

* * *

On her second day up from her sickbed, Miss Fortune announced that she was bored and wished to see new faces and hear new conversation. To Caroline's consternation, Sophia hit upon the idea of inviting Marcus Grant up to the house for afternoon tea.

'Not for a proper meal,' said Sophia, glad for something to divert Great-Aunt Martha from her hostess' shortcomings. 'We will just have a tea-tray and cakes.'

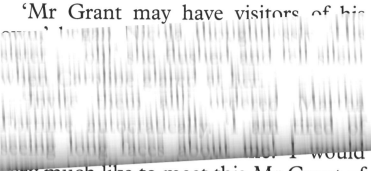

'Mr Grant may have visitors of his [illegible] I would very much like to meet this Mr Grant of yours! Now, come,' she added with a harsh chuckle, 'the doctor said you were to humour my whims!'

When Marcus Grant arrived with his sister and the beautiful Miss Dawes, Caroline was tempted to plead a headache and excuse herself from the tea-party. Yet she knew that Great-Aunt Martha would draw her own hateful conclusions from this. No — Marcus *and* his fair visitor must be faced. She marvelled at his being so thick-skinned as to accept the invitation at all. He knew that *she* had no desire to be socially civil to him!

The occasion passed off quite well, after all. Miss Fortune secured Marcus Grant at her side and left the family to entertain his lady visitors. Mrs Ratcliffe and Sophia talked together and this meant that Caroline and Nicola were obliged to converse with Miss Dawes.

The governess, Miss Patchett, was also present, as was David, but small Paula remained upstairs with Bessie. It was evident that Miss Patchett had known Miss Dawes before today and it seemed that she had no great opinion of the young lady. She merely gave a cool nod, then sat quietly talking to her young pupil.

Seeing that Caroline was uncharacteristically silent, Nicola strove to strike up conversation.

'You will see that I am properly dressed today, Miss Dawes,' she said. 'Oh, I do like your gown. *I* have never had anything so pretty, but then I am still more or less in the schoolroom.'

It seemed she had struck the right note. Alicia Dawes smoothed the soft blue silk of her gown with a loving hand and smiled at Nicola.

'Papa is so rich, you see,' she said in a

light, pleasant voice. 'It pleases him to buy me [illegible] Nicola next, when the visitor fell silent.

'Why, yes,' agreed Alicia sunnily. 'It is so convenient, you see! We are able to visit dear Marcus whenever we wish. He and I are such *great* friends,' she went on, 'and we have known each other *forever*!'

She prattled on, becoming quite animated upon the subject of Mr Grant. Then, inevitably it seemed, her talk went back to describing her newest gowns. It began to dawn upon Caroline that Miss Dawes might not be over-endowed with intelligence. The young lady appeared to have little conversation other than her absorption with clothes and *money*. Although Caroline liked a pretty gown as well as any other girl, she had never had Miss Dawes' intense preoccupation with wealth and what it might purchase. Indeed, the Fortune family had never been wealthy — even before Papa's death.

Caroline could see that Nicola's eyes were becoming glazed as she attempted to take in Alicia Dawes' description of her favourite ball-gown. In spite of herself, Caroline's lips began to twitch and, unaccountably, her spirits lightened. Marcus Grant caught her eye across Great-Aunt Martha's shoulder and one of his eyes twitched in faint suggestion of a wink. Scarcely able to credit what she had seen, Caroline gazed at him and was rewarded with another, more open, wink. Her cheeks took on a rosy flush and hastily she tried to help out Nicola in her one-sided talk with Alicia Dawes. Nicola had said that Marcus did not think highly of Alicia Dawes. She did appear to be rather an empty-headed girl! Yet, wait — there was always that unpleasant affair of the elopement to remember, she thought with a mental sigh.

Great-Aunt Martha brought the tea-party to [illegible] she went on. 'I enjoy his conversation!'

Marcus' look of astonishment made Caroline forget herself so far as to smile sympathetically. She was sure that he had spent the entire time in listening to Great-Aunt Martha and had scarcely even opened his mouth to reply!

He caught her smile and returned it conspiratorially. Although she could not completely forgive him, Caroline decided that it was impossible to dislike him heartily, after all. On coming to this conclusion, she found herself feeling happier than she had done for days.

Mrs Ratcliffe and Alicia Dawes left with Marcus, adding their thanks to his. It seemed that the ladies, at least, had enjoyed the afternoon.

'Such nice people!' declared Sophia with a beam of approval, when they had gone. 'I must say that Mrs Ratcliffe is a lady with whom I find I have much in common, even though she is so much younger than I. I quite enjoyed our talk!'

Martha Fortune ignored this remark. She stared pointedly at Caroline and said:

'Well, miss? And what do you think of the heiress? Her father is in trade and he is most ridiculously rich. His ambition is to buy his daughter a well-born husband, preferrably one with a title — a vulgar ambition, to my mind. However, it is possible that I am merely old-fashioned in my views! Well — how do you find her?'

'She is very beautiful and is a pleasant enough girl,' managed Caroline, wishing this speech had not been directed solely at her.

Great-Aunt Martha gave a cackle of laughter.

'Pleasant? Aye, Alicia is pleasant

enough, I'll allow. Who would not be *pleasant* with [illegible] Nicola [illegible] to her rescue.

'Mr Grant cannot be interested in Miss Dawes,' she said. 'Why — she would bore him to death inside a week!'

'I was not addressing you, child!' said Martha Fortune mildly enough. 'Ah — I have so enjoyed this afternoon! Perhaps we might repeat it soon?'

Sophia cast her a look of undisguised horror.

'How long do you intend staying with us?' she murmured faintly.

'Would you push a sick old woman from your door so hastily?' demanded Great-Aunt Martha affronted. 'I shall stay here, Sophia, until my health permits me to travel home! Now, where is that boy, Simon? His place is here with his family. I cannot understand all this modern gallivanting from place to place.'

'Simon is staying with friends, as you know,' said Sophia placatingly. 'I am sure he will return home before long.'

Great-Aunt Martha gave an unladylike snort.

'You have simply no *discipline*, Sophia,' she retorted. 'That is your main failing. You allow your children to run roughshod over you! Ah — things were very different in my day. Oh, by the way — I approve of your choice of governess, if of nothing else! She appears to be exactly what the children need.'

Miss Patchett had made good her escape with David, when the visitors left, so was unable to receive this rare tribute of praise from Miss Fortune's lips.

Caroline and Nicola were not able to discuss the tea-party privately until they were changing their gowns for dinner. Even then, very little had been said before Nicola changed the subject.

'Caro,' she said. 'When Great Aunt Martha [illegible]

[illegible] said Caroline with a groan. 'They will be caught for certain, Nico! Why, they are mere boys to be playing this dangerous game! They *must* be stopped! Do you know when this hold-up is planned to take place?'

'Y — yes,' said Nicola reluctantly, 'and it is too late for us to do anything at all. It is to happen this very night!'

Caroline gave her an impatient frowning look.

'I suppose you told Marcus all of this,' she said. 'I wish you had confided in me properly, Nico! I could have gone over to Channing House this morning and warned Simon that we knew everything. Now it is too late!'

'M — Marcus will stop them surely?' faltered Nicola. 'He knows it is arranged for tonight, for I told him.'

'He may forget!' said Caroline shortly. 'And even if he remembers, why must we be sure that he will do anything? What does it matter to *him* if our brother is convicted and hanged as a highwayman?'

Nicola bit her lip.

'Please do not talk like that!' she begged. 'I am sure Marcus cares enough about us all, to save poor stupid Simon! We *must* rely on Marcus, Caro! There is nothing else that we can do at this late date!'

Caroline gave her a long thoughtful look but said nothing.

13

At the time when Great-Aunt Martha was holding court at her tea-party at Fortune Hall, Simon Fortune was talking to his friend, Cedric, in the Channing library. He had been allowed to remain with the Channings, undisturbed, for several days now and was remarking upon this fact to his unresponsive friend.

'I am surprised that Mama has not obliged me to return home yet,' he observed with a grin. 'No doubt she is glad to have me absent, as the old lady is so ill. I had not expected to stay here so long without her grumbling at me to go back home again! Ah, well — it is all to our advantage, for me to remain here, is it not?'

Cedric hunched a thin shoulder moodily.

'If this great-aunt of yours is as

wealthy as you make out, then you'd be better served by going home and pandering to her whims,' he muttered. 'She's old, is she not? No doubt she'll die, one of these days. If I were you, Simon, I'd see to it that I was named in her will!'

Simon gave a hollow laugh.

'Oh, she is wealthy enough!' he agreed. 'However — she will leave nothing into my family. She hates us all, you see! You had the opportunity of judging her temper, the other night, Cedric! We could have been the most *desperate* of highwaymen — it would not have worried *her*! I suppose one should admire her courage in standing up to your pistol as she did! It was an odd quirk of fate that led us into stopping her coach! I nearly fell off my horse when I recognised *her* grim features glaring out of the window at us! Fortunately, her coachman is old and slow to take advantage, or he'd have realised we were somewhat at a loss, you and I. A younger man might have fired

at us and led to our identities being revealed. I could scarcely keep my face straight when Great-Aunt Martha described the tall, broad-shouldered villain that had bidden her stand and deliver! Her sight must be failing — though she'd never admit to such weakness! Anyway — why should I worry about inheriting *her* money? We have hit upon a splendid way of becoming rich! It is quite simple and is certainly profitable. The sight of that fearsome pistol soon causes a purse to change hands! Come, Cedric, what ails you today? I would have thought you'd have been filled with enthusiasm for tonight! This was all *your* idea, after all.'

Cedric Channing scowled.

'You are enjoying this, Simon — actually *revelling* in it!' he accused. 'Oh, lifting the odd purse here and there, is well enough,' he acknowledged grudgingly, 'but jewels are another matter! They are far too easy to trace and may prove to be our undoing. We still have those we took some time ago upon our hands. If we try to sell them, I am sure we will be done for! And if we cannot *sell* them — then what must we do? The longer we have them lying around here in my home, the more likelihood that they'll be discovered — along with our little evening jaunts! I have no wish to dangle from a hempen collar, even if you have, Simon Fortune!'

Simon gave him an incredulous look.

'You are *afraid*!' he jeered softly.

'Yes, I suppose I *am*!' agreed Cedric with a grimace. 'I have the oddest feeling, too, that Hubert knows exactly what we are up to! He will bide his time, though, before he acts. I know my dear brother's little ways! If *he* has found out about our game, then we are certainly in trouble!'

'Hubert?' scoffed Simon. 'You are starting at shadows, Cedric! Anyway, what would it matter if he *did* find out? He is your brother. He would not report you to a law-officer!'

'I wish,' said Cedric wearily, 'that I

had your confidence, Simon!' His voice became bitter. 'Hubert may well decide to report us — to Father, when he returns, at least, and remember that *he* is a Justice of the Peace! I wish we had never set out on this whole crazy business, Simon! Do you know — I have a mind to stay indoors tonight!'

'Tonight will be easy,' coaxed Simon. 'We will demand only money and say they may keep their jewels.'

Cedric gave a sniff of derision.

'Odd kind of highwaymen they'll judge *us*!' he retorted.

'What they think does not matter,' pointed out Simon patiently. 'It is how much they hand over that is important! Do not cry off now, Cedric! You were the one to get the information about the timing of this coach, after all. It would be a pity to waste your efforts!'

'Oh, very well,' said Cedric with an ill grace. 'I suppose one more little hold-up can do no harm!'

Simon might have been less confident of success tonight, had he known that their conversation had had an eavesdropper. Hubert Channing moved soft-footed out through the terrace door, a spiteful look on his thin-featured face. He had been listening from behind the very curtain which had sheltered Nicola Fortune the other day. Hubert was thinking hard of all he had just discovered. The fact that his younger brother was involved in doings of a criminal nature, worried him not one jot. His main interest was in calculating how much profit Cedric and Simon might already have made by their enterprising venture. There was little point in speaking out now, he decided. He had best wait and see how much tonight's haul was worth! He began to work out the best way to turn the situation to his own advantage.

By threatening to tell all to Father, he could demand a portion of the money stolen so far, to seal his lips. No — Hubert shook his head silently. It was too soon for that! He knew exactly what they were planning and this knowledge must suffice him for the moment. This, in itself, was a weapon in his hands!

Hubert emerged from the tangled roses upon the terrace and made for the stables. A man was standing in the entrance to the stableyard and Hubert could see immediately that he was not a Channing employee. The man had stiffened on sight of him, but made no attempt to leave.

'Arkwright!' said Hubert, ill-pleased. 'What are you doing? Who gave you leave to trespass here?'

'Good day, Mr Channing, sir!' said Will Arkwright, unusually subservient. 'I was wondering if happen there'd be a job going in t'stables, like? I'm a good man wi' horses, sir.'

Hubert sneered.

'Is that why you received quittance from your farm?' he enquired. 'I would say you were good for nothing, Arkwright!'

Will Arkwright approached suddenly and glared down at the slightly-built Hubert, huge fists clenching at his sides.

'Don't you come that tone wi' me, young sir!' he said threateningly. 'I could tear you limb from limb with one hand, if I had a mind to it!' Hubert fell back a step in alarm and Arkwright gave an unpleasant grin. 'Happen you'd do well to treat me wi' more respect,' he suggested. 'I know a thing or two about that young brother o' yours. Reckon he'd be in a mite o' trouble if I chose to speak up on what I know! Ah, yes! That makes you take a bit more notice, doesn't it, sir? Aye — I know what I know, see!'

Hubert stood his ground with an effort.

'My father would have you driven off his land if he could hear you,' he said blusteringly. 'You've no right to come here threatening me with your wild accusations.'

Arkwright gave a harsh laugh.

'Happen I know Sir Luke's safely from home!' he scoffed. 'An' what would you tell him, if he was standing right next to you, then? Would you say as how your young brother's playing a dangerous, unlawful game o' nights? Would you tell him that?'

Hubert cast a hunted look about him.

'What do you want of me, Arkwright?' he muttered, seeing no one to summon to his aid.

'Only a job, sir,' said the man with a wheedling smile. 'Now, don't back away! You an' I have a lot in common, think on!'

Trembling a little and despising himself for the weakness, Hubert Channing drew himself up to his full height, which was scarcely level with Arkwright's shoulder.

'What could *I* have in common with you — an evicted tenant-farmer?' he demanded, rage bolstering up his failing courage.

Will Arkwright gave him a considering look from his craftly little eyes.

'There's him as evicted me,' he said slowly. 'Happen you've no reason to like him either, young sir. He's done you no good in a certain direction!'

'You mean Grant?' asked Hubert with a doubtful frown. 'What reason have I for disliking him? I've never even met the fellow properly!'

'Happen there's the small matter o' Miss Caroline Fortune's — ah — affections,' sneered Arkwright, watching him closely. 'Aye — I thought that'd interest you!'

'Miss Fortune? What has she to do with Grant?' asked Hubert frostily.

Arkwright stared at him incredulously.

'It's plain enough to all concerned that you've lost your Miss Caroline to this same Grant as lost *me* my job an' my home,' he said. 'Can I put it plainer, sir? I thought you gentlefolk were supposed to be educated and intelligent, like? Even t'village daftie would know what I'm on about! Aye — we've something in common, young sir, like it or no. We've both cause to hate yon Grant fellow!'

Hubert gave a gasp of sheer outrage.

'I will not stand here bandying words

in discussing my private affairs with you!' he choked furiously. 'Get off our land, Arkwright! I would not give you a job even if I could do so. That is my father's province and I doubt he'd hire the likes of *you*! Try out your threats with him and let us see how far it gets you!'

Hubert Channing made good his escape, half-running across the stable-yard, in his haste to leave the vicinity of Will Arkwright and his insinuations. He did not even pause to weigh and consider what the man had dared to suggest. Doubts and suspicions about Caroline Fortune would come to plague him later. At the moment, he was only concerned with Arkwright and his effrontery in speaking in this loathsomely familiar manner.

The evicted farmer did not appear dissatisfied with his encounter with Sir Luke Channing's elder son, nor did he make haste to leave the Channing estate. He merely stared in Hubert's wake, a slow unpleasant smile crossing his face and his piglike eyes gleamed with malice.

'Reckon I've given that fine young cockerel something to think on!' he muttered to himself, as he finally turned to go.

14

Great-Aunt Martha was still far from well and the afternoon's social occasion had tired her more than she had expected. She sent Thwaite to her hostess with her regrets that she would be unable to dine with the family that evening. Once the elderly maid had returned to her mistress, Sophia Fortune gave a sigh of relief.

'Now we may be comfortable, my dears!' she said to her daughters with a smile. 'This afternoon went well enough, for she was kept occupied in talking to Marcus! I vow I was dreading having her undiverted attention upon myself this evening!'

'Mama — you sound glad that poor Great-Aunt Martha is not well!' chided Nicola. 'I think it is too bad of you!'

Sophia turned to her elder daughter.

'Caro does not blame me, do you,

love?' she said. 'Great-Aunt Martha was very *pointed* in her remarks about Marcus and that Alicia Dawes, was she not? I know that you did not like what she said, Caro, and I was pleased when Nicola stepped in to draw her attention. That was well done of you, Nico! Rudeness and lack of tact cannot be excused merely because your great-aunt is becoming old. Do you not agree, my love?'

Caroline started and stared blankly at her mother.

'Poor Caro has not the least idea of what you are rambling on about, Mama!' said Nicola with a disrespectful giggle.

'I — I am sorry,' murmured Caroline. 'I have a headache, Mama. I really cannot eat anything more.' She rose to her feet and pushed back her chair from the dining-table. 'You must both excuse me. I must go to my room now! Good night!'

Sophia Fortune stared wide-eyed, as her elder daughter left the dining-room, but Nicola frowned thoughtfully, as she peeled an apple.

'Nico,' said her mother suddenly, 'have I upset poor Caro with my thoughtless talk of Alicia Dawes? Although your sister will not admit it, she thinks very highly of Marcus. Can it be that she is *jealous* of his knowing this — this tradesman's heiress?'

Nicola shook her head uneasily.

'Mama, I feel you are wide of the mark,' she protested with an attempt at a smile. 'Caro could never be jealous of anyone — it is not in her nature. Certainly she would not be jealous of someone as boringly self-centred as Alicia Dawes, anyway! No — depend upon it, she is merely overcome with a headache, as she told us, Mama. Do recall all that time she has spent in waiting upon Great-Aunt Martha! No doubt she is feeling a sort of — of reaction from being freed from her duties!'

Her attempt to cover Caroline's abrupt leaving of the dining-table sounded rather far-fetched, even to Nicola's own ears. However, to her relief, Sophia nodded and accepted the explanation. Nicola was convinced that her sister's air of unhappy preoccupation was the result of pondering not upon Marcus Grant, but upon *Simon*.

Their brother's foolhardy behaviour must be kept from Mama at all costs, thought Nicola anxiously. With conscious effort, she began to talk about the afternoon's tea-party. Mama must not guess that anything was wrong!

'You liked Mrs Ratcliffe, did you not?' said Nicola, putting down her peeled apple, all appetite leaving her. It was very difficult trying to make light conversation with this dreadful knowledge of Simon upon her mind. 'Marcus' sister is not very like him in looks, is she, Mama?'

'Mrs Ratcliffe? Ah, yes,' smiled Sophia. 'We talked together for quite a while. She has been married for some time, but is still in close contact with her family. Apparently her home is not very far distant from here. Miss Dawes is an old friend and is visiting her at the moment. They have been coming to see Marcus quite regularly since he has taken up residence at the lodge. She seems a very pleasant young woman — Mrs Ratcliffe, I mean.'

'How did you find Alicia Dawes?' asked her daughter curiously.

Sophia shrugged.

'She is certainly a very beautiful young lady,' she allowed, 'and there is nothing about her which spells 'trade'. I am sure her gown must have cost a deal of money. However, she will not do for Marcus! I have decided we must secure him for Caro, love, and nothing must stand in our way!'

Nicola gave a soft, disturbed laugh.

'What does Caro say to this, Mama?' she murmured.

Sophia shook her head and frowned.

'Your sister is being very foolish about him!' she said severely. 'When she heard about his attempted elopement with Miss Dawes, she appeared to change her opinion of him entirely. She *says* she does not wish to know him now! Well — that unfortunate elopement affair occurred all of two years ago, Nico. If Marcus had any real feeling for that young lady — any *designs* upon her — then I am sure he must have had ample opportunity to ask her hand before now. No — depend upon it — his affections are not engaged in *that* direction. Caro has nothing to fear from Alicia Dawes!'

'Well, she did not try to talk with him this afternoon,' pointed out Nicola. 'Perhaps we must accept that Caro really does not *like* Marcus very much, Mama! It is too bad of you to try to match-make if poor Caro is unwilling!'

'Unwilling?' sniffed Sophia Fortune. 'I have eyes in my head, love! I saw Caro watching Marcus this afternoon *and* I saw the expression in her eyes!' She paused, then added dramatically: 'What is more, Nico, Marcus was watching *her*! I even saw him *wink* at her! There is more between the pair of them than we know!'

Nicola began to laugh with real amusement now.

'Oh, Mama!' she said. 'You are incorrigible! I, too, like Marcus Grant, but we cannot keep him bound to our family unless it is Caro's wish and *his* also!'

'Your sister should attend to her mother's wishes for once!' retorted Sophia. 'My mind is quite made up! Marcus Grant is the ideal husband for Caro! I am convinced he will speak up soon and we must make sure that the naughty girl gives him the proper answer to his suit!'

Unaware that she was under discussion, Caroline paced restlessly up and down her bed-chamber. She had been unable to eat or to talk in a normal manner, but was beginning to regret her precipitate leaving of the dining-room. Mama and Nicola would be convinced that she was ill! She only hoped that neither of them took it into their heads to look in on her before they retired to bed for the night.

Yet, nothing — not even the fear of discovery could overshadow the importance of what she must do. If Simon were caught tonight, then brought to trial — She brought her musings to an abrupt halt. The dreadful consequences of *that* must not be pondered upon!

My first difficulty, thought Caroline, as she began to unhook the gown she had worn for dinner, will be leaving the house undetected. Her hands stilled upon the fastenings of her gown. Marcus Grant had told Nicola that he would deal with Simon himself. If Nico had only confided in me sooner, thought Caroline wearily, I might have been able to have had a quiet word with Marcus on the subject this very afternoon. As matters stand, I cannot rely upon him to take action. Why — he might have forgotten completely that *this* was the appointed night! Also, thought Caroline, Marcus' manner of 'dealing' with her brother might only create new problems. No — Simon must be warned that she and Nicola and Marcus too, knew all that he and Cedric planned to do! He would not expect *her* to betray him, but he might anticipate *Marcus* informing the law-officers! Reluctantly, she went on to wonder how Marcus had intended to deal with the amateur highwaymen. Marcus Grant was still something of an unknown quantity. How far would his disapproval of Simon's youthful folly take him?

Caroline lifted her chin, stiffened her resolve and proceeded to don the clothing she had selected as being most suitable for the task in hand.

* * *

It was a dark, cloudy night, with only fitful rays of moonlight to illuminate the signpost at the crossroads. The local people had no use for this signpost even in daylight. They knew well enough where the four lanes led: one to the village; another to Fortune Hall; a third up on to the moors — soon deteriorating into a mere track. The fourth lane widened after its first few hundred yards and became a proper road. Anyone travelling far enough along this road would eventually arrive in the city of York.

A soft jingle of harness from beneath a cluster of trees on the moorland side of the crossroads, proclaimed the fact that the place was not entirely deserted at this late hour. Two horsemen were waiting there, concealed by the trees and conversing in low whispers.

'I tell you everything will go according to plan, Cedric,' muttered Simon Fortune, his eyes glinting with excitement through the slits in his black mask. 'It seems to me that a merchant driving home from York at this time of night is simply *asking* to be relieved of his purse!'

'If he hands over jewels, I shall throw them into the nearest ditch!' warned Cedric Channing in a sullen undertone. 'They are dangerous things to leave lying around the house. My father will be home soon, remember.'

'Don't spoil sport, Cedric!' pleaded Simon. 'We have done so well up to now — hush! Something is approaching!'

'It's early yet,' objected Cedric. 'Hold back, Simon! For the lord's sake do not ride out and challenge a lone rider! He may be a crack shot and *kill* one or both of us!'

Simon bit angrily on his lip. Cedric made a poor-spirited highwayman, he thought scornfully. He was convinced that his sister, Nicola, would make a better partner at this game!

'It *is* a coach, Cedric!' he breathed triumphantly. 'Right? Pistol at the ready!'

Just as the coach lumbered up to the crossroads on the road from York, the two amateur highwaymen rode out of the shelter of the trees, straight into its path, with loud cries of 'Stand and deliver!' Usually they had found these tactics to cause great confusion, with the horses slewing the coach sideways off the road and the coachman kept well occupied in controlling them. Tonight was different. This coachman reined in swiftly and competently and the horses drew to an abrupt halt with a deal of noise but a minimum of disorder. Cedric levelled his pistol at the coachman and Simon rode round to the side of the coach. He was alarmed and disconcerted to find that the window had already been lowered and that a burly, red-faced man was steadily pointing a pistol up at him.

At this moment, unnoticed by the rest of them, another rider arrived at the crossroads and hesitated under the trees. The moon chose to reveal itself just then and Cedric Channing gave a sudden, panicking intake of breath and shouted:

'It's a trap! That's no coachman! It's *Grant* up there on the driver's box! Run for it!'

Simon, who was unarmed, lunged wildly at the passenger's pistol with his riding-whip and made off into the night with all good speed. Cedric was less fortunate. He wheeled his horse too sharply and it reared madly at the exact moment when a shot was fired from the pistol that had suddenly appeared in the hand of the cloaked coachman.

Had Cedric's horse responded in the manner in which he had intended, the shot would have passed harmlessly over his head. As bad luck had it, his rearing mount lifted him upwards into the path of the bullet.

Cedric Channing gave a piercing scream of pain and shock as his horse galloped off wildly in Simon Fortune's wake — Cedrick half-lying across its neck.

Gradually the sound of thudding hooves died away then, suddenly, the clouds moved completely away from the moon, so that it shone down brightly upon the stationary coach. As the driver leaped down into the road and the passenger made his exit from the coach, a slightly-built figure on a great black horse cantered out from beneath the trees.

'You *shot* him!' the driver was accused in a shocked, disbelieving voice. 'Marcus Grant — you arranged this *deliberately*! You knew that Cedric and Simon would be waiting here for a coach and you saw to it that *this* coach arrived first! You cold-bloodedly shot a young boy whose only crime was a thirst for adventure! You are despicable!'

The coachman, who was indeed Marcus Grant, strode across purposefully and grasped the black horse's bridle.

'Dismount, Nico, love!' he ordered firmly. 'I am sorry that you had to witness this unfortunate affair. Why did you not stay at home like a good girl? I told you that I would deal with the matter.'

'You certainly *did* deal with it!' choked the girl in the saddle. She clapped her heels furiously against the black horse's sides. 'Home, Hermes!'

'Ah, not so fast, young Nico!' said Marcus calmly. Effortlessly, he scooped the struggling girl down from the saddle and held her firmly against him, somehow managing to retain a grip upon Hermes' reins.

With a sudden nod to the man who had been the coach's passenger, he tossed him the reins and cradled the slender figure of the girl in his arms. Poor little Nico, he thought ruefully. How like her — to put on her breeches and ride out on her beloved horse to warn her foolish brother that his plans were no longer secret! Silently, he cursed Cedric Channing's idiot horse for rearing just when he fired a would-be warning shot over the boy's head. There was little hope now that this escapade could be kept quiet. Sir Luke Channing was a Justice of the Peace. He would go to any lengths to discover how his younger son had come to be injured — Marcus hoped fervently that he *had* only winged the boy. Before long, it seemed likely that this whole sorry tale would be public knowledge.

Marcus gave the girl in his arms a hug

and rested his cheek against her tangled fair hair.

'Better now, Nico?' he asked gently when he felt her shudder and give a small sob.

Suddenly she thrust him from her and glared up at him from defiant, tear-wet blue eyes.

'I am *not* Nico!' she said flatly. 'I shall hate you as long as I live for what you have done tonight, Marcus Grant!'

Marcus grasped her quickly by the shoulders and held her so that she could not turn from him.

'*Caroline*?' he said sharply. 'What the *devil* are you doing out at night in Nico's breeches and riding Nico's horse?'

'D — don't you swear at *me*, Marcus Grant!' she said angrily. 'Nico told me all about Simon and Cedric and so I rode out to warn them, but I was too late — too late for poor Cedric!' she finished with a sob.

Suddenly moved to anger, Marcus Grant gave her a shake.

'If you think I came here tonight with the intention of deliberately injuring a young boy, then you are wide of the mark,' he said curtly. 'Now — get back on that horse, Caroline! I will escort you home!'

She stared up at him, her face white in the moonlight. Then she bit her lip and cast her eyes round for something to serve as a mounting-block.

'Well?' demanded Marcus with an impatient frown. 'What are you waiting for, Caroline?'

The coach-passenger spoke up at last. He sounded both interested and amused, which was unforgivable in the circumstances, fumed Caroline.

'Happen she can't get up into t'saddle on her own, Mr Grant,' said the man with a grin. 'T'horse is a mite high for her, see?'

Marcus' brow cleared and he gave a short laugh. Without hesitation, he picked her up in his arms and tossed her up into the saddle. With a swift movement, he divested himself of his enveloping coachman's cloak and threw it to his companion with a nod and a word of thanks for his aid that night. Effortlessly, Marcus mounted behind Caroline, easing her forward on to the horse's neck. One firm arm clamped about her waist and the other reached round her to grasp the reins. With a final word of farewell to the other man, who was already preparing to drive the coach away, Marcus turned Hermes' head down the lane to Fortune Hall.

Caroline tried mutinously to pull away from him, but he held her firmly, his breath warm upon her cheek. For the first time, she became aware of the impropriety of her being abroad at this hour, in *breeches* and alone with a *gentleman*. She gave a gulp and bit back a childish desire to weep.

'M — Marcus, will you t — tell Mama about this?' she whispered.

'Oh — so I am *Marcus* again, am I? Do you really hate me, Caroline?' he said in her ear, slowing Hermes down to a walk.

Her back stiffened against him.

'Why d — did you have to *shoot* at Cedric?' she wailed suddenly. 'You knew who he was! You knew he was not a real highwayman!'

'I aimed over his head — *well* over his head,' said Marcus evenly. 'I had the notion that he was preparing himself to shoot *me*. The lad was armed, Caroline — or did that escape your notice? I had no idea that his horse would rear at that moment.' He paused, then repeated firmly: 'Do you hate me, Caroline?'

'Oh, Marcus — I just do not know,' she said unhappily. 'Oh, please take me home!'

Marcus gave a sudden chuckle.

'If your mother could see us now, she would be convinced that we were eloping!' he observed. 'Will you be able to get back into the house unobserved, love? I think I will be able to smuggle Hermes back into the stable. If Whitton does catch me, I'll think up some tale or other and not give you away!'

Caroline twisted round to stare

uncertainly into his face. He no longer sounded angry with her, in fact he seemed to be treating her as a fellow conspirator.

'I left the terrace door unlocked,' she admitted. 'I will let myself in very quietly. No one will hear me. Nico's room is next to mine and she sleeps like the dead — oh! Marcus — what about poor Cedric? You do not think you killed him, do you? What are we going to do about him?'

'*You* are going to do nothing more tonight!' said Marcus. 'I will ride over to Channing House as soon as I have stabled Hermes.'

She allowed herself to be reassured. He walked Hermes quietly up the drive of her home, dismounted at the rose-terrace and put out his arms to her. After only a brief hesitation, she dropped down lightly and was held firmly in his arms. Marcus put his lips briefly to her brow then released her.

'Don't hate me, love,' he murmured, 'for that would set all my plans awry!'

Before she could find words to answer this strange remark, he had left her and was leading Hermes off into the darkness. The door was unlocked as she had left it and Caroline tiptoed into her house, her heart thudding. Marcus' words were throbbing in her mind and a warm glow crept over her, blotting out even the shocking incident that she had so recently witnessed at the crossroads.

Then, with a start, realisation struck her. For all his gentle words, Marcus Grant was still the same man who had eloped two years ago with a heiress and was still upon friendly terms with that same young lady.

With a suppressed sigh, Caroline reached her bed-chamber door and halted. She slipped inside quickly and began to undress in the dark. Dropping her sister's shirt and breeches upon a chair, she reached for her night-robe. Tomorrow, she supposed she must confess to Nico that she had borrowed not only her 'working clothes' but also her horse!

Wearily she climbed into bed. Tired though she was, she lay sleepless for some considerable time, as she pondered worriedly on how badly Cedric Channing might have been injured. Yet, for all this, her last waking thoughts were with Marcus and his plea that she must not hate him.

15

'Caro! Wake up, love! Do you feel better now?'

Reluctantly, Caroline opened her eyes to greet the new day. Her eyelids felt leaden and she had difficulty in focussing properly upon her sister.

Nicola sat down heavily on the edge of the bed. She began to laugh.

'You are not ill,' she observed with relief. 'We were quite worried about you last night and we thought we had best let you sleep today until you were ready to wake up! You look ghastly, love,' she went on with a cheerful lack of tact. 'No one would guess that you had slept for quite fourteen hours. Why — you still look unrefreshed!'

Caroline gave a groan and sat up slowly against her pillows.

'What time is it, Nico?' she said and gave a vast yawn.

'Well — you missed breakfast and you will miss luncheon, too, unless you get out of bed this instant!' chided Nicola. Suddenly her eyes fell upon the chair beside the bed and they widened incredulously. 'My breeches!' she gasped. She jumped down from the bed and picked them up, then turned accusing eyes back to her sister. 'Oh, *Caro*! You wore them last night,' she said mournfully. 'There is no other explanation! You went out to warn Simon and you did not tell me! Caro — how *could* you?'

Caroline threw back the bed-coverings and climbed out slowly.

'You are right, of course, love,' she admitted. 'Yes, I wore your breeches last night *and* I rode Hermes, too! You wouldn't have expected me to drag my poor old slug of a mare out from her warm stall at night, would you? Now — don't preach at me, Nico, or reproach me either! I just *had* to go out to the crossroads and it would not have done for both of us to have gone.'

'What happened?' asked Nicola, forgetting her air of grievance. She dropped the breeches and sat down upon the bed again. 'Did you stop Simon and Cedric Channing from robbing that coach? Did you see Marcus Grant? Oh — do tell me, love, before I *burst* with curiosity!'

Caroline gave a sigh.

'It was all very unpleasant and not a grand adventure at all, Nico,' she said soberly. 'Yes, I will tell you what happened, but you must not let Mama know. Don't say a word to her! Promise?'

'I promise,' agreed Nicola, wide-eyed.

'I was too late to warn Simon,' she began quietly. 'When I arrived at the crossroads, he and Cedric had already halted the coach. I stayed under the trees and watched.'

'What happened then?' breathed Nicola, when her sister paused. 'Did you see Marcus? He said he would stop the boys himself.'

'Yes, I saw him,' nodded Caroline

with another heavy sigh. '*He* was driving the coach! He planned matters so that they would halt *him*. He — he fired over Cedric's head, but Cedric's horse reared and he was hit. Both he and Simon rode off. I know no more than that.'

'Marcus *shot* Cedric Channing?' asked Nicola with an incredulous frown. 'Oh — this is dreadful, Caro! It is all my fault that Marcus knew anything of this planned hold-up. If I had not told him, he could not have shot Cedric! Will they h — hang him?'

'Hang whom?' asked Caroline blankly, turning from the mirror where she was brushing the tangles from her fair hair. 'The authorities cannot hang anyone without evidence, love! Neither Cedric nor Simon were apprehended last night.'

'I — I meant *Marcus*,' explained Nicola, giving her sister a troubled look. 'If Sir Luke finds out that he shot Cedric and if — if Cedric dies — '

Caroline shuddered.

'Nico, love!' she begged. 'Let us

change the subject! Perhaps the worst is over. One thing is sure. Marcus Grant will have achieved his aim. I am certain that neither Simon nor Cedric will have the heart to plan highway robbery again! I think their days as highwaymen will be over!'

Nicola gave her a doubtful look.

'Did Marcus see you, love?' she asked next.

Caroline nodded.

'He saw Hermes and the breeches and thought at first that I was *you*! He was very angry with me for being there and — and he brought me back home,' she finished lamely.

Nicola looked at her searchingly.

'Oh,' was all she said.

'When he left me,' went on Caroline hastily, 'Marcus intended riding over to Channing House to find out how badly Cedric was injured. That, Nico, is the full story, I promise you!' she ended, trying to smile.

'You will be going down to the lodge after luncheon to see Marcus and find out what happened,' said Nicola. 'Please say that I may go with you, Caro?'

'Certainly you shall,' agreed Caroline. 'But for you, we would not have known anything of last night's planned hold-up.' It would be a relief not to be obliged to face Marcus alone yet, she owned privately. 'Come — I am ready, at last! Let us go in search of luncheon, love. I vow I am vastly hungry!'

'So you should be — riding round the countryside all night long!' reproved her sister with a grin.

When they reached the dining-room, they found Great-Aunt Martha at the table with David. She frowned when the young ladies joined her, but neither felt that an apology for tardiness was due. Luncheon was an informal meal. Barnes always set out bread and butter, fruit, coffee for the adults and milk for the children. Those who wished to partake, helped themselves. Those who were not requiring refreshment, did not need to come to the dining-room at all.

When Caroline and Nicola seated

themselves at the table, David was chatting in a lively manner to his unappreciative relative.

'You should just see Soppy beg for a biscuit,' he said, pouring out his milk and spilling a little as he did so. 'He is a *capital* little dog! I wish he could be mine! Oh — I am learning to ride again,' he beamed suddenly, setting down his cup in a manner which made his great-aunt wince and cast her eyes heavenwards.

'You are learning to ride, love?' put in Caroline quickly, before the old lady could voice a reprimand and spoil the child's pleasure. 'I did not know that.'

'Yes,' said David. 'Nico knows, don't you? It is really Quimby's idea. He is a *capital* fellow, you know! My leg does not trouble me half as much as it did before and no one could possibly be afraid of that fat old pony! Mr Grant and Quimby say that when I can ride properly, they will bring Mama down to the stableyard, so that I can surprise her. Now, don't tell her yet,' he smiled confidently at Great-Aunt Martha and his sisters, 'for it is to be a surprise!'

Cheerfully, he gulped down the rest of his milk and left the room with an apple in his hand. Great-Aunt Martha glared balefully after him.

'That boy used to be a quiet amenable child,' she grumbled. 'I fear he has changed — and for the worse! I remembered him as a docile, obedient boy and now — '

'He used to be so withdrawn and unhappy,' defended Nicola. 'That accident to his leg affected him badly. Since Marcus came, David has changed — for the *better*, we think! He has stopped having those horrid nightmares and has even lost his fear of riding. Yes, he is a changed boy but we are happy with the change!'

Angry colour rose in Great-Aunt Martha's shrunken cheeks.

'You are a pert chit!' she retorted tartly. 'In my young days, you would have been sent to your room immediately for daring to voice your opinion in that forward, impudent manner. And,' she added, with a scowl for Nicola's look of wide-eyed innocence, 'I believe, miss, that I have seen you in the stableyard, clad in *breeches*!'

'Breeches?' echoed Nicola without a blink. 'Oh — I am sure you must have mistaken Whitton for me, Great-Aunt Martha. He works in the stableyard and *he* wears breeches!'

The old lady gave her a look of disgust. Then she turned to Caroline and smiled:

'Now, you are a *lady*, my dear!' she said approvingly. 'It would never occur to *you* to parade yourself in men's clothing. Your sister is a hoyden!'

Nicola gave a choke of laughter and quit the room in a hurry, leaving Carloine to bear the full brunt of the old lady's conversation. Being naturally polite and considerate, she talked to Great-Aunt Martha for a further quarter of an hour, although inwardly she was pleading for release, so that she could go to the West Lodge to question Marcus Grant.

'You are a good girl!' said her elderly relative and nodded at what she judged to be her great-niece's modest blush. 'I feel you are by far the best person in this haphazard household! Now — run along, my dear, for I must not keep you tied here with a tiresome old woman like myself.'

This subtle remark had the desired effect in ensuring that poor Caroline stayed at her side for a further twenty minutes or so. Thus, it was mid-afternoon by the time the two sisters were able to leave the house.

* * *

'Cedric is not badly injured,' said Marcus Grant reassuringly, once his visitors were seated and Quimby had been dismissed from the room. 'The bullet merely grazed his upper arm and I feel he was frightened rather than hurt.'

'He gave a most terrible scream,'

recalled Caroline with a watery smile. 'I was convinced that you had killed him, Marcus!'

Nicola pulled a face.

'I wish I had been there!' she declared. 'I missed all of the excitement!'

Marcus shook his head reprovingly, but he was looking at Caroline's pale face and the shadows beneath her blue eyes.

'Simon is to return home today,' he said. 'He is much chastened and actually *thanked* me for taking charge at Channing House, last night. I arrived there shortly after the two boys. Cedric was in something of a state and bleeding badly — '

'I thought you said his injury was slight?' put in Nicola indignantly.

'Surface wounds often bleed a lot,' reassured Marcus. 'Simon was stabling their two horses when I rode up and both of the beasts were in a nervous state. Cedric was propped up against a bale of hay. I am afraid I treated them like a couple of naughty children. I even tucked young Cedric into his bed like a fond Mama!' finished Marcus with a reminiscent chuckle.

Caroline frowned.

'Surely they must have blamed you for shooting at Cedric?' she protested doubtfully. 'But for you they would have achieved yet another robbery. I know my brother better than you do, Marcus! He will not take your interference lightly!'

'Cedric told me that Simon forced him to go out last night,' said Marcus quietly. 'I am afraid that Simon has been the leading-light in this partnership. However, I am convinced that last night subdued even *him*.'

Nicola gave a sigh of relief, although Caroline still looked doubtful.

'Then everything is all right,' declared Nicola. 'Simon will come home. No one will ever find out that he and Cedric have been playing at being highwaymen.'

Marcus shook his dark head slowly.

'Things are not quite so simple,' he said. 'I rode over to Channing House again this morning, to check upon Cedric's wound. Allowing a servant to tend him, would only lead to suspicion and questions, you see.' He paused, then went on: 'Cedric had hidden a quantity of stolen jewellery in his room. The boys had shared out the money they had taken, but they found jewels impossible to dispose of — not being professional thieves,' said Marcus with a faint smile.

'Oh dear — has Sir Luke returned and discovered the jewels?' asked Caroline. 'Must everything come out into the open? Is that what you fear, Marcus?'

He shook his head.

'The jewels,' he said simply, 'have disappeared!'

The girls were unable to discover more at this point, for Quimby entered the room and announced in an expressionless voice:

'Sir — Mrs Ratcliffe and Miss Dawes

have just arrived. Shall I show them in here?'

Marcus muttered something beneath his breath. Fortunately it was inaudible, thought Caroline, heartened by the fact that he did not appear to be overjoyed at the prospect of a further meeting with Alicia Dawes.

The visitors entered the room. Mrs Ratcliffe nodded amiably at Caroline and Nicola, but Alicia Dawes merely stared at them with wide-eyed astonishment.

'Marcus, dear,' said his sister without preamble. 'I have just discovered that a friend of James' lives quite close to here. He is Sir Luke Channing. I wondered if we might all,' her friendly nod included the Fortune sisters, 'drive over and pay a call upon him.'

For once, Marcus Grant appeared to be lost for words. Caroline decided to break the ensuing silence before it became remarked upon.

'Sir Luke is a friend of your husband?' she managed. 'How small the world is, to be sure!'

Mrs Ratcliffe nodded.

'I know that he has two sons,' she said. 'Poor Alicia has not been well,' she added with a reproachful look for Marcus. 'I have taken her beneath my wing for a time, you see, and am endeavouring to introduce her to new young people, to brighten her spirits.'

'Poor Alicia' frowned at her friend and, in spite of herself, Caroline felt a twinge of sympathy for the young lady.

'Sir Luke is from home,' revealed Nicola hastily. 'I do not feel it would be at all convenient for us to visit Channing House until he returns.'

'Oh,' sighed Mrs Ratcliffe regretfully, 'then Alicia must wait awhile before she meets his charming sons!'

'Yes, I am afraid that she *must*,' put in Marcus smoothly. 'Miss Fortune and Nicola were about to leave and return home and it is time that I made my daily tour of the estate. May I show you to your coach, ladies?'

'But we have only just arrived,

Marcus!' protested Alicia.

Caroline was taken aback with the ease in which Marcus Grant shepherded his unwelcome visitors from the room and she did not miss the scowl directed upon herself by the normally pleasant Alicia Dawes.

When Marcus came back into the room he gave an appreciative chuckle.

'My sister is a born matchmaker,' he said. 'I wonder which of Sir Luke's 'charming' sons she has selected for Alicia? Once Wingate Dawes has met that rascal Cedric and — ah — Hubert,' with a sidelong glance at Caroline, 'he will whisk his beloved daughter speedily from the neighbourhood!'

'Hubert will be *Sir* Hubert one day,' said Nicola unthinkingly, 'and Great-Aunt Martha says that Mr Dawes — oh!' Her hand flew to her mouth and she went pink.

'Precisely!' nodded Marcus, with a twinkle in his dark eyes. 'But even a *title* will not redeem Hubert if Wingate Dawes learns Cedric's little secret, for he has no room for *ramshackle* families!'

Caroline decided to turn the subject.

'You said those jewels had disappeared,' she reminded him.

'The jewels?' repeated Marcus blankly. 'Ah, yes — the *jewels*! Simon went to check upon them in their hiding-place and found them gone. He and Cedric suggest that Hubert has a hand in this. Cedric assures me that he is convinced Hubert knows all about this highwaymen affair.' Marcus spread his hands. 'There, my dears, appears to lie our problem! Hubert Channing is something of an unknown quantity to me. I cannot judge his reactions.'

'He is *horrid*!' said Nicola vehemently.

Caroline lifted her chin stubbornly.

'I am sure Cedric will have nothing to fear,' she said. 'Surely you do not think that Hubert would betray his own brother to the authorities?'

'I am sure that he *would*!' retorted Nicola.

Marcus was watching Caroline closely.

'There is always the chance that it was *not* Hubert who removed those jewels,' he pointed out. 'The important thing is — who knew about them and *why* were they taken? I told you that Simon was subdued,' he reminded the sisters. 'This new development has shaken him. Both he and Cedric are hourly expecting to be denounced to the authorities. That is why I must discover the whereabouts of those jewels,' he ended quietly. 'They may have been taken as a weapon against the boys.'

Caroline dropped her eyes.

'You should not put yourself into further danger on Simon's behalf,' she murmured. 'He has been foolish and I suppose he must bear the consequences, sir. It is scarcely *your* concern.'

'It is not?' murmured Marcus, giving her an enigmatic look. 'Ah — well that remains to be seen!'

16

'I am flattered that you should decide to return home for the last day of my visit, young sir!' said Great-Aunt Martha sarcastically to Simon. 'One might be excused for wondering if you have been avoiding my company.'

'I would not be so ungallant as to confess to that, ma'am,' murmured Simon.

The family were seated at the dining-table, together with Miss Patchett who had joined them on this last occasion before Martha Fortune's departure on the morrow.

'Your sojourn with friends does not appear to have suited you,' pursued Great-Aunt Martha suddenly, with a sharp look at the shadows beneath Simon's blue eyes. 'I declare you seem to have lost weight, boy! some — take another portion of this excellent pie.'

She turned to her hostess with a look of approval. 'I must say that you eat well at Fortune Hall, Sophia. Indeed, I am quite favourably impressed with the way you go on — with one or two minor exceptions, may I add! I was convinced you would be all to pieces! Your governess,' with a nod to Miss Patchett, who inclined her own head gravely in return, 'has brought much-needed order to the younger members of the family. I cannot like David's new boisterousness of manner but I can find little fault otherwise on this score. Poor, dear Henry would have been proud of his family,' she ended in an uncharacteristically sentimental tone.

'We knew you would approve of what Marcus Grant has done for us,' put in Nicola eagerly. She gave her sister a sidelong glance and added wistfully: 'I wish we could keep him in our family!'

Great-Aunt Martha frowned at her severely.

'I really cannot commend Nicola's pert manner, Sophia,' she reproved. 'As for Mr Grant — he appears to manage your affairs adequately but anything more than a business-arrangement with that gentleman is not to be countenanced. It would be *most* undesirable!'

Honoria Patchett set down her napkin with an air of purpose and looked steadily across the table at the old lady.

'Why do you say that, ma'am?' she asked, her voice deceptively mild. 'You speak as if you know something to Mr Grant's discredit. I wish you would explain yourself.'

Martha Fortune gave vent to a sound suspiciously like a snort.

'This Marcus Grant is nothing but a fortune-hunter,' she declared. 'Why — two years ago he eloped with Wingate Dawes' daughter. *She* is quite an heiress, may I add!'

Miss Patchett primmed her lips.

'Nonsense!' she said forthrightly.

Sophia and her daughters widened their eyes with shock at the governess' dismissal of Great-Aunt Martha's claim.

Simon lost the air of abstraction he had brought back with him from Channing House and gave a grin of unholy glee. It seemed that a sparring-match was about to commence! His blue eyes flicked from one to the other of the elderly ladies. *My* money goes on the governess, he thought with disrespectful mirth.

'Oh dear!' murmured Sophia unhappily, preparing to step in and mediate.

Caroline put a hand on her mother's arm and frowned her into silence. Miss Patchett was obviously very sure of herself. Was she about to throw new light upon that very matter which had plagued Caroline incessantly?

'I *beg* your pardon?' said Great-Aunt Martha frostily.

Honoria Patchett was not in the least put out.

'Alicia Dawes is a forward little hussy,' she remarked calmly. 'Poor Mr Mark showed her a degree of polite friendliness some two years ago. Why should he not have done so, for she was his sister's friend? On her Papa's orders, she was to seek out personable young men of good birth, then parade them for his approval. Yes — it was not quite the thing,' admitted Miss Patchett, 'but Wingate Dawes has amassed a vast fortune and Miss Alicia is his only child. He makes the assumption that money will pave the way for anything! He is determined that his daughter shall marry into one of the best families in the land but knows that his own — ah — origins make it difficult to secure her a *title*. Miss Alicia became convinced that Mr Mark would fit Papa's bill! Now, Mr Mark would not tell you this himself, for fear of appearing ungallant but he *fled* to Scotland to escape the young lady's embarrassing attentions!'

Caroline found her voice suddenly.

'They — they did not elope together?' she asked doubtfully.

Honoria Patchett gave her a reassuring smile.

'I have this from Mr Mark's own lips, my dear,' she said, 'and *what* he will say to me for betraying his confidence, I cannot imagine! However, I will go on. Miss Alicia packed a bag, appropriated one of her father's coaches and shamelessly pursued Mr Mark! Fortunately an *elopement* did not suit Wingate Dawes and *he* pursued his daughter! The rest you will know. Miss Alicia put about this tale of an elopement and Mr Mark, being a *gentleman*, did not seek to embarrass her by issuing a contradiction!'

'To think that he is still civil to her after all of that!' said Nicola indignantly. 'I wonder that Mrs Ratcliffe should continue to bring her to visit Marcus so frequently. He cannot like it at all!'

Honoria Patchett gave a dry cough.

'I feel that Mrs Ratcliffe is blinded by her friendship with Miss Alicia. Between the pair of them, they are determined to catch poor Mr Mark in the matrimonial net!'

Great-Aunt Martha had listened to all of this in silence — a remarkable feat for her, thought Simon, grinning to himself.

'There is a certain ring of truth to what you have told us, Miss Patchett,' admitted the old lady eventually. 'Yet — to my mind, Alicia Dawes is a featherhead! I doubt she has the *initiative* to stage a mock elopement.'

'I feel we must credit her with nothing more than a desire to follow her Papa's wishes to the letter,' said the governess. 'When Wingate Dawes showed his disapproval of her pursuit of Mr Mark, Miss Alicia obediently lost all interest in him! We must set the blame for this renewal of acquaintanceship at Mrs Ratcliffe's door, I fear!'

'I *knew* that Marcus did not like her above half!' crowed Nicola triumphantly.

'Nicola!' reproved her mother, forestalling both Great-Aunt Martha and Miss Patchett.

'Grant is not such a bad kind of fellow,' allowed Simon unexpectedly, distracting attention from his sister's fall from favour. 'The estate is beginning to show signs of paying for itself, now that the farms are properly run and there is rent coming in from the South Lodge. I hope Grant will agree to continue here until I come of age. I feel I can learn much from him!'

He succeeded in drawing a battery of incredulous eyes upon him and had the grace to look down.

'It seems,' said Martha Fortune with a stiff smile, 'that I am no longer needed here! I am sure you will do very well without me. However — my mind is made up on one point. Miss Patchett sees a bright future for David, she assures me. I believe he is now strong enough in his health to hold his own at a good school in the near future. I intend to make myself financially responsible for the boy's education.' She glared round the table. 'There is to be no opposition from any of you. I will have my way!'

Sophia thought over this proposition and gave a slow nod.

'Provided that David himself is in

agreement with going away to school, I cannot see anything for us to quarrel over,' she said. 'Indeed, we shall be indebted to you, ma'am!'

* * *

Great-Aunt Martha was upon the point of departure next morning, when Simon burst into the house, his face white with shock.

'A — a highwayman held up a c — coach at the crossroads last night!' he stammered.

'That is not possible!' gasped Nicola. 'Simon — it cannot be true!'

Great-Aunt Martha gave Simon a penetrating stare.

'Why should this news meet with such astonishment on your part?' she enquired of him. 'We all know that the man who held up *my* coach is still at large. Very likely it is the same hulking fellow!'

'V — very likely!' agreed Simon hollowly.

In general conversation of farewells and wishes for a safe journey, the highwayman was forgotten. Miss Fortune's coach bowled off down the gravelled drive and David and little Paula ran alongside waving until its speed overcame them.

'So she has gone!' remarked Sophia in tones of extreme satisfaction. 'There, my dears, I *told* you it would all turn out well, did I not?' she added with a fine disregard for truth.

Purposefully, Caroline and Nicola followed their brother and eventually cornered him on the rose-terrace.

'Oh, *Simon*! You *promised*!' wailed Nicola. 'It is too bad of you!'

Simon stared at her uncomfortably, in no doubt of her meaning.

'Nico — I never left the house last night!' he protested. 'You saw me at the dinner table with your own eyes.'

'You could have easily slipped out later, when we were all asleep,' pointed out Caroline.

'Well, I did not!' retorted Simon,

stung by this show of sisterly accusation. 'I promised Grant I was finished with being a highwayman. Now — do not be putting the blame on Cedric either,' he said in a hurry. 'He was injured last time and it will be a long while before *he* ever sets foot out of doors in the dark again, for *any* reason!'

'There was never a highwayman in this district until *you* began your little game,' said Nicola, unconvinced. 'One thing is certain, brother mine — Marcus will set the blame fully on your shoulders! You will have trouble making him believe that you are innocent!'

'I tell you it was not me!' reiterated Simon in mounting alarm.

'Then,' demanded Nicola unanswerably, 'who *was* it?'

On the persuasion of his sisters, Simon went to the West Lodge to discuss the matter with Marcus Grant. Not unnaturally, Marcus seemed inclined to disbelieve his protestations of innocence.

'Whatever I may be,' said Simon

heatedly, 'I am not a *liar*, Grant! I gave you my word I would never hold up another coach and I have not done so!'

Marcus regarded him in silence for a moment, then he gave a nod.

'Very well, Simon,' he said. 'What of Hubert Channing, then? Could it be that you put the idea into his head and that he has taken up your trade — always supposing that he knew what you and his brother were about? Could that be the explanation, do you think?'

Simon's brow cleared and he laughed with real amusement.

'Hubert Channing?' he said. 'Hubert playing the highwayman? No — I am afraid we cannot blame Hubert! Why — he'd be constantly in fear of spoiling the set of his coat. The fellow's a curst *dandy*!'

'Who took those jewels, if not friend Hubert?' asked Marcus. 'I feel we cannot dismiss the notion entirely, Simon!'

Simon took heart from that 'we' and diffidently asked if he might accompany

Marcus on his daily tour of inspection.

'I may as well learn all I can from you,' said the boy with a wry grin. 'After all, Grant, the estate will be mine one day and I know very little about how to run it! Also,' he hesitated, 'I feel I owe you something. But for you, I could be threatened with the hangman's noose! I may have made a poor highwayman but, maybe, with practice I may become a good kind of landowner!'

Marcus Grant said nothing more to Simon on the subject of the highwayman's exploit. He made up his mind to investigate the matter personally. This time, he thought ruefully, he must ensure that neither Caroline nor Nicola were aware of his intentions!

17

Marcus Grant stifled a yawn and leaned over to pat the neck of his patient mare. Up to now, his self-imposed vigil had proved fruitless. This was his third night of waiting beneath the trees at the crossroads. Not for the first time, he wondered if Simon Fortune's changed manner had been merely assumed. Was the boy as grateful as he professed for Marcus' intervention in that last hold-up? Could it be that Simon was playing a devious game of his own? Had the boy played highwayman yet again, knowing that his family's guardian would feel obliged to investigate, thus losing several nights' sleep? Marcus had to admit that he did not yet know Simon well. Surely that air of contrition and friendliness had not been entirely assumed?

Suddenly, Marcus sat up alertly in the

saddle as his sharp ears caught the sound of an approaching vehicle. In all probability it would pass harmlessly by, he thought. However, there was the chance that this might prove to be the night when a masked figure would ride out into its path and force it to halt. Even as Marcus leaned forward, his eyes straining to pierce the darkness, he became aware that he was not alone. His mare gave a prancing side-step, sensing the presence of another horse.

'Reckon I'll make sure of you this time, my fine gentleman!' hissed a voice in his ear.

He was too unprepared to avoid the crushing blow which descended on his head and pitched helplessly from the saddle. Not completely unconscious, he felt rough hands upon him and guessed that his pockets were being searched. Something rough was passed about his face to be secured painfully in the region of his wound. If it were meant as a gag, then it missed its target, being bound across his eyes and not his mouth. He heard soft movements of withdrawal and knew he was alone.

The next thing he became aware of was a jumble of sound, which seemed to come to him through a choking fog now threatening to envelope him. Searing pain gripped him but grimly he clung to consciousness. He heard the harsh grating of coach wheels, the shrill whinneying protest of sharply reined-in horses and, above it all, a strident voice calling out: 'Stand and deliver!'

Something about that voice touched a chord of remembrance. Marcus groaned helplessly, tried to lift his head, then was swamped in blackness. He knew nothing of the hold-up taking place only yards from where he lay.

The masked figure pocketed a purse held out by the coach's angry passenger, wheeled his mount about and made for the trees. The flying hooves narrowly missed the still figure of Marcus Grant. Although the highwayman appeared to be unhurt, he suddenly gave vent to a loud cry of seeming pain, then galloped off into the night up the moorland track. The unconscious man's mare fled in panic in his wake.

A shot was fired from the coachman's box, booted feet clattered on the road's rough surface, then cautiously approached the trees. Marcus Grant's eyes flicked blankly open as a twig cracked almost by his ear. He groaned once more.

'Over here!' came a triumphant cry. 'Reckon you were right, Jacob! You said as you heard him cry out! Must have hit his head on a branch, like! We've got him, see!'

A booted foot rolled Marcus helplessly on to his side.

'Aye,' exhulted another voice. 'We've got him — masked an' all! Happen we'll see this 'un dangle in York afore long!'

Dimly Marcus Grant became aware that he was being carried out from the shelter of the trees. He opened his mouth to protest at his rough handling but no sound came. When he was thrown carelessly on to the floor of the coach, he experienced fresh waves of pain before merciful oblivion claimed him.

* * *

Hubert Channing rode swiftly up the drive of Fortune Hall, his horse churning up the gravel. He rode round to the stables, dismounted and threw the reins to Whitton with a curt word. Then, unannounced, he strode into the house and demanded to see Simon.

'I will see if Master Simon is at home, sir,' said Gregory in dignified reproof.

The footman's impassive eyes took in the unusual fact that Mr Channing's wig was awry and he was startled to find himself pushed aside by this normally well-mannered gentleman.

Hubert marched purposefully to the foot of the stairs.

'Simon!' he shouted. 'Where the devil are you?'

The drawing-room door opened

abruptly and Caroline put out an uncertain head.

'Hubert!' she said, her blue eyes startled. 'Whatever is the matter?'

Hubert Channing drew in an excited breath.

'I must see Simon,' he declared more moderately. After a moment's thought, he added: 'Something has happened. It concerns you all but I must see Simon first.'

When Simon was eventually found and brought to the drawing-room, he eyed Hubert Channing morosely.

'Well, and what ails you, Hubert?' he asked.

Hubert Channing cast Caroline a frowning look before speaking.

'Oh — very well! She will have to know this sooner or later, I suppose!'

'Is it the jewels?' said Simon, losing his ill humour. 'Never tell me that your father has come home and found the jewels?'

Hubert shook his head impatiently.

'It's Grant,' he said. 'Your dear family

guardian has been arrested! I just heard the news so I came over to tell you. I knew you would all be interested!'

Caroline sat down suddenly in a chair.

'M — Marcus has been arrested?' she gasped. 'But — what happened, Hubert?'

Mr Channing shot her a half-triumphant look.

'I knew from the first that he was not a gentleman,' he said. 'It seems he is nothing but a common highwayman! Well, last night he held up his last coach. He fell off his horse and was captured!'

'I — I do not believe you, Hubert,' managed Caroline, her face pale as she gripped the arms of her chair. 'Marcus is not a highwayman. You are talking nonsense!'

'He was caught wearing a mask and his pockets were full of jewels,' said Hubert maliciously. 'What explanation is offered, save that he is a highwayman?'

Simon gave a sudden exclamation.

'I have it!' he shouted. 'The fool! The

idiotic *fool*! I have the unpleasant feeling that I know exactly how this came about — except for the mask and jewels part. Marcus must have been investigating. I should have guessed he would do so! It is so like him!'

Caroline rose unsteadily to her feet, clasping her hands hard to stay their trembling.

'Hubert — where is he?' she said quietly. 'Where have they taken Marcus?'

'Oh — he will be in prison in York, I expect, awaiting trial,' said Hubert Channing carelessly.

'This is all my fault,' uttered Simon with a groan. 'My fault and Cedric's.'

Hubert grinned unfeelingly.

'I know all about that little lark,' he admitted. 'Use your head, Simon, and keep quiet. Grant will be blamed for the whole of this affair and then, when he has been — '

He fell silent, his narrowed eyes on Caroline, who shuddered and became even paler. Simon gave an exclamation of fury. His fist shot out and caught

Hubert Channing a glancing blow upon the chin. Hubert staggered backwards and his wig fell off. Snatching it up and cramming it back upon his shaven head, he snarled:

'You'll regret doing that, Simon Fortune!'

Simon drew himself up to his full height, topping Hubert by at least two inches.

'Get out of my house, Channing!' he grated, taking a forward step.

Hubert Channing backed to the door, fumbled for the handle and fled. When Simon turned triumphantly to his sister, he found to his dismay that she was lying in a swooning heap upon the carpet. Lifting her into a chair and holding down her head, he shouted for Barnes, cursing Hubert Channing beneath his breath.

* * *

The days which followed were unhappy ones. Mr Brown, tenant of the South

Lodge, departed for York, taking Simon with him at the boy's own insistence. Quimby set off to High Crags with the unenviable mission of explaining the position to Marcus Grant's family. The manservant left the pup, Soppy, in the care of young David. Mabel Brown was alone at the South Lodge, until Nicola recalled her presence and had her brought up to the house.

Caroline appeared to have entered a world of her own. For two days, she neither ate not spoke, just stayed upon her bed, staring unseeing up at the ceiling. In the end, it was Miss Patchett who broke through her unnatural wall of silence. The governess marched into Caroline's room with a bowl of soup and began to spoon it purposefully into the girl's mouth. For a moment, there was no reaction. Then, as the soup began to dribble down her chin, Caroline came into indignant life.

'Miss Patchett! What are you about?' she gasped.

The governess set down the soup bowl and clasped the girl firmly to her bosom.

'Now, Miss Caroline,' she said fiercely, 'you are going to *weep*! I order it!'

The held-back tide of anguish broke its banks as Caroline obligingly obeyed this demand. She sobbed on against the hard yet comforting shoulder then gasped and fell silent when her face was suddenly bathed with an extremely cold wet towel.

'She'll do now,' said the governess briefly across her shoulder to an anxious-faced Nicola.

Slowly, Caroline sat up on the edge of the bed.

'Marcus?' she whispered. 'Is he — ? Did they — ?'

'Mr Mark is quite well, according to Mr Brown,' reassured Honoria Patchett. 'You cannot help him by getting yourself into this state, my dear!' she added severely. 'Naturally he is innocent of that ridiculous charge — the problem is in proving him to be so.'

'I was frightened for you, Caro, love,' admitted Nicola, sitting down beside her sister. 'I thought you were going into a *decline*!'

Miss Patchett sniffed.

'Miss Caroline is by far too sensible to indulge in hysterical behaviour,' she said roundly. 'Her illness was brought on by shock. It is not unusual for it to happen in this way.'

Caroline pulled herself together with an effort.

'I think I am hungry,' she said wonderingly.

Nicola gave a relieved smile.

'Well — there is no soup left, love!' she said. 'Miss Patchett poured most of it over your gown!'

'Nicola — you will help your sister to put on a clean gown,' said the governess firmly. 'I will go down to the kitchen and order her a light, sustaining meal. Come, Jacob!'

The little dog, who had been sitting unnoticed at her feet, followed her out of the room, with a goggle-eyed look at the girls.

'Has any progress been made in proving Marcus' innocence?' asked Caroline at the dinner table that evening. Her cheeks were pale and her eyes unnaturally bright, but her relieved family judged her to be recovered from her recent indisposition. 'What is being done for him?' she demanded.

'My Albert's gone back to York wi' Master Simon to be wi' t'young gentleman,' said Mabel Brown quietly. 'Mr Grant reckons as someone hit him first then put yon mask on him and t'jewels in his pocket. Stands to reason *he* never put them there himself!'

'Has Marcus any idea who did this to him?' asked Caroline with commendable steadiness. 'Could it be the same man who shot him when he first came here?'

Her mother shook her head wearily.

'We can only guess what happened, my love,' she said. 'All we can do now is wait — and hope.'

Caroline stood up abruptly, all appetite leaving her.

'I will *not* just sit back and wait for news that Marcus has been h — hanged!' she declared. 'There must be something we can do — questions we can ask, perhaps, in the right quarter?'

'Mrs Fortune is right, my dear,' said Honoria Patchett regretfully. 'At a dreadful time like this, we women are powerless. We must pray that right prevails!'

'Nico,' said Caroline mutinously, when the girls were alone together later. 'I cannot just *wait*! There must be something we can do. Think hard, love!'

Nicola bit her lip, her blue eyes troubled, then she nodded.

'Hubert Channing,' she said slowly. 'Could he know more than he revealed? Certainly he has no reason for liking poor Marcus. Yet, would he hold his tongue on vital information that might *save* Marcus?'

'Hubert,' said Caroline candidly, 'is

capable of being utterly despicable!'

Determined to pursue any avenue, however dubious, in the quest to prove Marcus Grant's innocence, Caroline rode over to Channing House next morning. She went alone, for Nicola was at her schoolroom tasks.

She found the Channing brothers together in the library. Cedric was very pale and his left arm was in a linen sling. Hubert glared when the servant admitted Caroline.

'Did you arrange this, Hubert?' she demanded without preamble. 'Come, answer me! A man's life is at stake.'

Hubert Channing sneered. He made no pretence of misunderstanding her meaning.

'Come to beg for his life, have you, Caroline?' he asked unpleasantly. 'Do you think I would lift a hand to help Grant? However — since you ask me so nicely — no, I arranged nothing. Does that answer you? Go home — I've had a full sufficiency of your family!'

Cedric stood very still and gave his

brother a look of pure dislike.

'We have been discussing this matter, Caroline,' he said, ignoring his brother's black frown. 'Hubert thinks Will Arkwright is at the bottom of this and I am inclined to agree with him. Arkwright found out about Simon and me. He threatened Hubert, saying he would tell Father about our playing highwayman — '

'Hold your tongue!' rapped Hubert angrily. 'It's no concern of hers!'

'Why should I be silent?' retorted his younger brother. 'I've nothing against Grant — for all he put a bullet through me! Caroline — we think Arkwright took the jewels from my room. It would have been no difficult task as we are not exactly overstaffed with servants! We think he planted the jewels upon Grant — arranging to have him caught with them in his possession. I'll lay he knocked Grant out and then put that mask on him.'

'Guesswork, little brother!' sneered Hubert Channing. 'Well — do what you will with Cedric's fabrications, Caroline, but I fear you'll be too late to save Grant from the hangman's noose!'

He was speaking to empty air, for Caroline had made her exit through the open door on to the rose-terrace. Once back in the saddle, she turned her mare purposefully in the direction of the village.

Reining in to a mere walk, she made her way towards the smithy and was rewarded by the sight of Will Arkwright lounging outside on a bench in the sunshine.

'Arkwright!' she shouted at him.

The man started, then shuffled to his feet and looked up at her, shading his eyes against the strong sunlight.

'Why — Miss Fortune has come a-visiting,' he said with a harsh laugh. 'An' what can a poor out o'work farmer do for you, my dear?'

Caroline lunged forward with her riding-whip and cracked its leather thong about the man's powerful shoulders.

'What can you do for me?' she

repeated angrily. 'You can own up to your villainy! Get yourself to York, Will Arkwright, and testify to Marcus Grant's innocence — that's what you can do!'

Arkwright moved swiftly for one of his bulk and took the whip from her hand with contemptuous ease. He threw it down on to the road and gripped her mare's bridle.

'An' who' been telling you fancy tales about me, young missy?' he hissed.

'Hubert Channing!' said Caroline. 'It seems he knows all about you!'

Arkwright released the bridle and grinned.

'That young cockerel?' he said and spat sideways into the dust. 'A word from me an' he'll sing another tune. Aye, he'll withdraw whatever he told you quick enough when I've done wi' him.'

Caroline urged her mount forwards and galloped off down the village street, tears stinging her eyelids. It could well be that Cedric Channing had told her the truth about Arkwright, but what good was that knowledge to her? How could she help Marcus without solid proof to back up her claim?

She left her mare with Whitton and went wearily into the house to find that Simon had returned from York.

'Simon?' she said. 'Why are you here? Why are you not with Marcus? Have you left him to bear all of this alone?' she accused him.

'Brown is at the prison still,' explained Simon. He was travel-stained and his face wore a grim expression. 'Things look bad,' he admitted, 'but I've discovered something. Before Marcus was struck down, he heard a voice. He told me last night that he's convinced the man was Arkwright, Caro!'

His sister nodded.

'I have just accused Arkwright to his face,' she confessed and told Simon all that had happened that morning.

'Arkwright will make a move now,' said Simon thoughtfully. 'I am sure of it.'

'He will go to Channing House and threaten Hubert into silence,' said Caroline heavily. 'Simon — there is no way of making Arkwright talk and set the noose about his *own* neck.'

'We will see about that!' declared Simon. 'All is not lost, love!' Clumsily he bent and kissed his sister's cheek. 'Make my excuses to Mama, Caro — I must go!'

'Where are you going?' she asked him blankly. 'Back to York?'

'No, love,' said Simon. 'I am going to Channing House. If Arkwright turns ugly, they may need my help.'

'Take care — ' began Caroline in alarm, but Simon had gone.

He rode swiftly down the road to Channing House, tethered his horse to a bush outside the front entrance and banged impatiently at the door until an elderly manservant wheezed up to admit him. Pausing only to enquire of Cedric's whereabouts, he marched into the house.

'Simon,' said his friend in some relief.

'I thought you might come. Did Caroline tell you what we suspect?'

Simon gave a grim nod.

'Where is that dandified brother of yours?' he said. 'We've got to make him see that he has nothing to fear from Arkwright. Caro is convinced that one word from that lout will seal Hubert's lips forever! Why — this thing has nothing at all to do with your brother! Arkwright is merely seeking his revenge because Marcus Grant evicted him from the farm. It is very likely that he was the one who shot at Marcus earlier. But it has *nothing* to do with Hubert. What can *he* lose by telling the truth?'

Just as Cedric opened his mouth to reply, a sudden loud report echoed through the house.

'W — was that a shot?' asked Cedric uncertainly. Then his eyes widened. 'It came from the library!' he gasped. 'I left Hubert there. Surely Arkwright has not crept into the house and *shot* my brother?'

They raced breathlessly to the library,

flung open the door, then froze with shock at the scene before them. Hubert Channing stood beside the library table, white-faced and with a smoking pistol held in one trembling hand. Across the threshold of the garden-door slumped the inert figure of a heavily-built man.

'It's Arkwright!' breathed Simon.

'Hubert — you shot Arkwright,' said Cedric in a stunned voice.

Hubert Channing turned haunted eyes upon them and the pistol dropped with a sudden clatter from his nerveless hand.

'Yes,' he agreed tonelessly. 'I shot him.'

He swayed on his feet, then pitched forward in a dead faint, leaving Simon and Cedric gazing in fascinated horror at the ominously still figure in the doorway.

18

Will Arkwright was dead, shot through the heart by the panic-stricken Hubert, who had armed himself with the pistol on the chance of receiving an unwelcome visitor. He had meant only to frighten the fellow, he protested when he returned to his senses.

Having fobbed off the servants' curiosity with the tale that they had been fooling around and that the pistol had gone off accidentally, Simon and Cedric were left with the problem of disposing of Arkwright's body, in a manner which suggested no connection with Channing House.

Hubert retired to his bed and was no use to anyone, condemned Simon scornfully. There was little point in expecting help from *that* quarter.

The plan concocted to rid themselves of the embarrassment of having a corpse upon their hands, was a somewhat involved one, but resulted in a success which exceeded all they had dared hope to achieve.

For the remainder of that day, Arkwright's body was dragged out on to the terrace and hidden beneath the tangled roses. When darkness fell, the plan was put into operation. With the aid of Simon's horse, the corpse was transported to the crossroads, a roughly-fashioned mask about the dead face. Urgency had overcome all natural squeamishness, even on Cedric's part. Faithfully copying Arkwright's own earlier scheme, they deposited him beneath the trees, halted the coach which obligingly presented itself, induced the enraged driver to fire, then made good their escape, in the hope that Arkwright would be judged to have died at that moment at the coachman's hands.

Amazingly enough, the plan worked. As an added bonus to their success, the coach proved to be that of Cedric's own father, returning home at last. Sir Luke Channing, being a Justice of the Peace, instigated a full-scale investigation of the villain who had dared to attempt to rob him. Amongst Arkwright's possessions at the village smithy, was discovered a leather purse belonging to a certain Mr Hetherington — supposedly robbed recently by one Marcus Grant.

At this point Cedric and the younger members of the Fortune family felt it was safe to inform Sir Luke of this conclusive proof of Marcus' innocence. *Arkwright* must have robbed poor Mr Hetherington, they urged, then sought to avenge himself for eviction by involving Marcus Grant. Why — the fellow had already attempted to kill poor Mr Grant once, by shooting at him! There seemed no reason to suppose that anyone else held a grudge against Marcus, so it seemed natural to lay the blame for this earlier attack at the door of the dead Arkwright. The young people had little difficulty in convincing Sir Luke of the truth of all that had taken place in his absence. Speedily and efficiently, the Justice of the Peace set in motion all that was necessary to secure Marcus Grant's release from prison.

* * *

'Mr Mark is due home this evening, miss,' Quimby informed Caroline with a joyful beam. 'Justice has been done and it is all over at last!'

'Perhaps I could wait?' asked Caroline. 'I — I must see Marcus as soon as he arrives.'

Quimby frowned and shook his head doubtfully but Caroline remained firm.

'I will do very well on the couch here in the sitting-room, Quimby,' she said definitely. 'I promise not to be a nuisance.'

She sat down to prove her intention of staying and the pup, Soppy, grown larger now, bounded over and put his heavy head upon her knees, gazing up at her from soulful brown eyes. Grumbling to himself and warning that her wait might prove to be a lengthy one, Quimby left her with the dog. An hour went by and dusk began to fall. Caroline moved to the window and stared out for a moment at the neat little garden. Here was just one more small sign of all that Marcus had done for her family, she thought with her lip quivering. He had almost paid for this with his life! Somehow she would make it up to him, she promised herself fiercely. She went back to the couch and sat down, then put up her feet and wrapped her gown about them. If her wait was to be a long one, then she might as well wait in comfort, she decided. In a very short time she was asleep.

When Quimby put a disapproving head around the door to light the candles, he saw that the young lady was fast asleep with the ungainly pup sprawled heavily across her lap. The elderly man gave a sudden smile and quietly left the room.

Caroline opened her eyes with a start, blinked at the brightness of candlelight and found Marcus Grant kneeling beside the couch, his face only inches from her own. Giving an exclamation of joy, she obeyed her first impulse which was to throw her arms about him, bursting into tears as she did so.

'I believe,' suggested Marcus after a moment, 'that we would manage better, love, if we removed this large lump of dog!'

Soppy gave a wriggle and inserted his hairy head between them, proceeding to lick both of their faces with impartial enjoyment. Suddenly, Caroline pushed aside both Marcus and the dog and rose to her feet, her hands flying upwards to tidy her hair.

'Oh,' she said wretchedly, 'my gown is crumpled and I am *covered* in dog hairs! But I have waited so long for you — ' she faltered.

'Not half as long as I have waited for you, love!' retorted Marcus with a mischievous grin. 'When you first put those huge blue eyes upon me I was quite undone! Why else would I have decided to play nursemaid to your family?'

Caroline frowned at him.

'I remember that day very well,' she said indignantly. 'Hermes had thrown poor Nico. I was standing by helplessly and you scowled at me in *such* disapproval.'

Marcus raised a dark brow at the dog.

'The lady stands in need of convincing, Blenkinsop,' he observed.

Without warning, he took Caroline into his arms and kissed her thoroughly.

'Caro — I *love* you!' he declared rather less steadily. 'This unpleasant affair is now at an end and we can be ourselves again. And — ' he held her away from him and glared at her fiercely, 'if you tell me you dislike me then I will call you a liar!'

He kissed her again, so that she was unable to say a word.

'But what about poor Alicia?' she asked him dazedly, when she was again able to speak.

'Poor Alicia?' scoffed Marcus. 'I did myself a good turn by being thrown into prison, love! Wingate Dawes heard all about it. He dislikes scandal and has removed his daughter from my vicinity — permanently, I trust!'

'Oh,' murmured Caroline, beginning to relax. 'Marcus,' she said a little later, 'do not be angry with Simon, will you? He just had to play the highwayman once more! You must agree that he and Cedric did their best for you in the end.'

'How could I be angry with Simon?' said Marcus magnaminously. 'I must keep on the right side of that brother of yours, if I am to beg him for your hand!'

Caroline gave a soft chuckle.

'He is only a boy,' she said. 'You need not ask him — *Marcus*!' she added in realisation. 'Do you really wish to m — marry me, after all the trouble my family has caused you?'

Marcus did not appear to heed her words.

'I am your guardian,' he decided with

a comical grin, 'therefore I need ask no one's permission, other than my own. Thus — I give myself my full consent to marry you, love!'

Although there was no opposition on this score from either Caroline's or Marcus' own family, the marriage was unavoidably delayed by a brief period of mourning. Great-Aunt Martha had suffered another heart-attack and this one proved to be fatal.

To the astonishment of all, she had willed her entire estate, with the exception of a bequest to her maid, Thwaite, to 'my beloved great-niece Caroline Fortune — the best of a feckless family.'

'The best? Ah, yes — I second that!' said Marcus with a smile.

THE END